293977
19.00
Woiwode   Oct93
Silent passengers

DATE DUE			

Silent Passengers

ALSO BY LARRY WOIWODE

What I'm Going to Do, I Think 1969

Poetry North: Five Poets of North Dakota 1970

Beyond the Bedroom Wall 1975

Even Tide 1977

Poppa John 1981

Born Brothers 1988

The Neumiller Stories 1989

Indian Affairs 1992

Acts 1993

Silent Passengers

❉ Stories by

Larry Woiwode

Atheneum
New York 1993

Maxwell Macmillan Canada
Toronto

Maxwell Macmillan International
New York Oxford Singapore Sydney

Copyright © 1993 by Larry Woiwode

Most of these stories first appeared, in different form, in the following publications: Antaeus, Antioch Review, Image, The New Yorker, Paris Review, and Partisan Review.

Atheneum   Maxwell Macmillan Canada, Inc.
Macmillan Publishing Company   1200 Eglinton Avenue East
866 Third Avenue   Suite 200
New York, NY 10022   Don Mills, Ontario M3C 3N1

Macmillan Publishing Company is part of the
Maxwell Communication Group of Companies.

Library of Congress Cataloging-in-Publication Data

Woiwode, Larry.
    Silent passengers: stories / Larry Woiwode.
        p.   cm.
    ''Atheneum fiction.''
    ISBN 0-689-12159-8
    I. Title.
    PS3573.O4S57   1993
    813'.54—dc20   92-39648

10 9 8 7 6 5 4 3 2 1

Printed in the United States of America

Book Design by Ellen R. Sasahara

For
Stephen & Wanda

down many roads

Lifting one's head, one could see up there,
between the top branches of the trees,
a river of sky flowing.

—Jules Renard

Contents

Silent Passengers

❧ Wanting an Orange

Oh, those oranges arriving in the midst of the northern winters of the forties—the mere color of them, carried through the door in a net bag or crate from the white winter landscape. Their appearance was enough to encourage my brother and me to start thinking it might be time to develop an illness, which was the surest way to receive a steady supply of them.

"Mom, we think we're getting a cold."

"*We?* You mean, you two want an orange?"

This was difficult to answer or dispute; the matter seemed beyond our mere wanting.

"If you want an orange," she would say, "why don't you ask for one?"

"We want an orange."

" 'We' again. '*We want an orange.*' "

"May we have an orange, please."

"That's the way you know I like you to ask for one. Now, why don't each of you ask in that way, but separately?"

"Mom . . ." And so on. There was no depth of degradation we wouldn't descend to in order to get one. If the oranges hadn't made their way north via some conveyance by Thanksgiving, they were sure to arrive before Christmas, stacked first in crates at the depot, filling that musty place, where pews sat back to back, with a springtime acidity, as if the building had been rinsed with a renewing elixir that set it right for another year. Then the crates would appear at the grocery store, often with the top slats pried back on a few of them, intoxicating us with the resinous smell of splintered wood, in addition to the already orangy atmosphere that foretold the season more explicitly than any calendar.

And in the broken-open crates (as if burst by the power of the oranges themselves), one or two of the spheres would lie free of the tissue they came wrapped in—always purple tissue, as if that were the only color that could contain their nestled populations. The crates bore paper labels at one end—of an orange against a blue background or a blue goose against an orange background—signifying the colorful otherworld, unlike our wintry one, that these phenomena had risen from. Each one, stripped of its protective tissue, as vivid against the purple as a pebbled sun, encouraged you to envision a whole pyramid of them in a bowl on the dining-room table, glowing in the light, as if radiating the warmth that arrived through the windows from the real winter sun.

And all of them were stamped with blue-purple names as foreign as the otherworld you might imagine as their place of origin, so that on Christmas day you would find yourself digging down through everything else in your Christmas stocking, as if tunneling down to China, in order to reach the rounded bulge at the tip of the toe that meant you had your hand on one— another state of existence, wholly separate from your own, placed here by the providence of your parents' hands like a shining baseball.

The packed heft and texture, finally, of an orange in your hand—this is it!—and the eruption of smell and the watery fireworks as a knife, in the hand of someone skilled, such as your mother, goes slicing through the skin, so perfect for slicing.

This gaseous spray can form a mist like smoke, which can then be lit with a match to create actual fireworks, if there is a chance to hide alone with a match (matches being forbidden) and the peel from one. Sputtery ignitions can also be produced by squeezing a peel near a candle, at least one of which is generally going or going out at Christmastime, and the leftover peels can be set on the stovetop to scent the whole house.

And the ingenious way in which oranges come packed into their globes! The green nib at the top, like a detonator, can be bitten off, as if disarming the orange, in order to clear a place for you to sink a tooth under the peel. This is the best way to start. If you bite at the peel too much, your front teeth will feel scraped, like dry bone, and your lips begin to burn from the bitter oil. Better to sink a tooth into this greenish or creamy depression and then pick at that point with the nail of your thumb, removing a little piece of the peel at a time. Later, you might want to practice to see how large a piece you can remove intact. The peel can also be undone in a continuous ribbon, a feat that maybe your father is able to perform, so that after the orange is freed, looking yellowish, the peel, rewound, will stand in its original shape, though empty, of course.

The yellowish whole of the orange can now be divided into sections, usually about a dozen, by beginning with a division down the middle; after this, each section, enclosed in its papery skin, will be able to be lifted free or torn loose more easily. There is a stem up the center of the sections like a mushroom stalk, but tougher; this can be eaten.

A special variety of orange, without any pits, has an extra growth, or nubbin, like half of a tiny orange, tucked into its bottom. This nubbin is nearly as bitter as the peel, but it can be eaten, too; don't worry. Some of the sections will have miniature sectional reproductions embedded in them and clinging for life, giving the impression that babies are being hatched, and if you should happen to find some of these, you've found the sweetest morsels any orange can provide.

If you prefer to have your orange sliced in half, as some insist upon, the edges of the peel will abrade the corners of your mouth, making it feel raw as you eat down into the white of the rind (which is the only way to do it) until you see daylight through the orangy bubbles composing the peel's outer side. Your eyes might burn; there is no proper way to eat an orange. If there are pits, they can get in the way, too, and the slower you eat an orange, the more you'll find your fingers sticking together. No matter how carefully you eat one, or bite into a quarter, juice can always spray or slide from a corner of your mouth; this happens to everyone. Close your eyes to be on the safe side and for the eruption in your mouth of the slivers of watery meat, which should be broken and rolled fine over your tongue for the essence of orange. And if indeed you've sensed yourself coming down with a cold, there's a chance you'll feel it driven from your head—your nose and sinuses suddenly opening—in the midst of the scent of a peel and eating an orange.

Oranges can also be eaten whole, rolled into a spongy mass and punctured with a knife or a pencil (if you don't find this offensive) and sucked upon. Then, once the juice is gone, you can disembowel the orange as you wish, eat away its pulpy remains, and eat once more into the whitish interior of the peel, which scours the coating from your teeth and makes your numbing lips and the tip of your tongue tingle and swell up from behind, until, in the light from the windows (shining through an empty glass bowl), you see orange again from the inside. Oh, oranges, solid *O*s, light from afar in the midst of the freeze, and not unlike that unspherical fruit that first passed from Eve to Adam and from there (to abbreviate matters) to my brother and me.

"Mom, we think we're getting a cold."

"You mean, you want an orange?"

This is difficult to answer or dispute or even to acknowledge, finally, with the fullness that the subject deserves, a fullness that each orange bears, within its own makeup, into this hard-edged yet insubstantial, incomplete, cold, wintry world.

✿ A Necessary Nap

Is there anything in my life, even my inner life, as perverse as this? Gilian wonders, watching his four-year-old, Will, on his back in bed, buck over the stuffed animals his mother has gathered around him. Getting to her knees next to the bed, she replaces a rabbit and an elephant.

"Anne," Gilian says, in a rising inflection of warning. He doesn't believe she's firm enough with the boy, so she has called him upstairs to enforce this nap. Gilian moves to a corner and crosses his arms, blinking against the sunlight on the ceiling—which slants so near his head it warms his bald spot—and refuses to be moved, much less lose his temper. He remembers reading somewhere that parents should never express anger toward their children at bedtime. That could mean most of the day, in Will's case, he thinks, and is wearied at the thought that he has read too much.

Anne pushes back her hair, long and springily coiled at its ends, and sits on the edge of the bed. She reads a children's book aloud, then places it on the slippery pile of a dozen she's finished, on the floor at her feet. She draws Will into her lap and sings, rocking him from side to side, the third time she's done this. Gilian helplessly yawns. She lays Will down. He sits back up. She turns him on his stomach and he rolls from side to side, then he's up and crawling until his head bangs the wall. Gilian takes him by a bare foot, as he might a lamb, and pulls him flat.

Crying won't get Will his way, Will knows by now, so he shrieks and tries to slide out of bed. Gilian turns him on his back, and Will reaches up and yanks at an ear. Gilian puts his palms on Will's shoulders and holds him down, firm but detached. Submit, he thinks, unable to understand his son's resistance to sleep, since it's the only time Will doesn't have to listen to them. A four-year-old's world!

He stares into Will's eyes, past irises of interleaved silver and blue, and tries to smile, fighting back an irrational fear that the boy is possessed. He senses Will give with this—still on his back, one arm flung up over the bed, his broad and dimpled hand relaxed—and sees his features soften in a first surrender to sleep. Gilian regrets his anger this morning, when he shouted at Will for his foolishness with a sled outdoors. He wonders if it's proper to stare at the boy like this as he goes under. He looks up at Anne and thinks, We know his face better than ours—it's the mirror we study from any angle we choose. Every act of his is at our mercy. She dimly smiles.

Will's eyelids tremble, slices of white flickering under his brushy eyelashes, and the color in his face fades with his sudden heavy breathing, more labored than after a run, as if he's been stricken and is breathing his last.

Gilian rises, releasing his pressure, cautious, and Anne gives him a grim nod of accomplishment—this has taken an hour— and then bends over Will and covers him with his tangled bedclothes. She runs a hand over his hair, blond but starting to blacken at its roots, and Gilian thinks of how, until this summer, Will preferred to remain in the house with her and help with the work here. But since the summer he has wanted to be outdoors with Gilian—riding the machinery or fetching tools or feeding with baby bottles the lambs that the ewes refuse to accept.

Anne leans and kisses Will's forehead, and curves and loops of shadow, like projections of her darkest thoughts, swarm over the slanted ceiling above the bed, then slide away in reverse as she stands. She tiptoes off, starting to relax as she nears the door, and Gilian can empathize with her over this "daily trial," as she has come to call Will's nap.

"Do trees sleep?" Will has asked.

Now he sleeps. Feathery fingers, like hundreds of his mother cleaning a window, flutter at the edges of the darkness he drifts under. Past it he watches the other side of life, released by sleep, enter the rooms of the house. The house is him. Bare roads longer than any road he has seen uncoil in a movement like a song—not like the way they lie flat under a car—and the emptiness of the sky opens around on all sides. Layers of cold arrive in colors that turn into a candy cane held by a sniffling lion. Its nose looks bigger than Dad's tractor. It leans and licks the fingers from the window until his mother is gone.

"Ah!" the boy cries, and Gilian and Anne, settling into their chairs in the living room below, look up. Gilian lays the *Times* that arrives a day late over his lap, and in the scouring sun reflected from a snow-laden spruce beside the window, he can see creases beneath Anne's eyes. He wants to smooth these. She opens a book on the arm of the chair and places her chin in her hand, her index finger pinning her hair at her temple, and Gilian waits for her to sense the directness of his attention. She was the one who wanted to live in the country, for Will's sake, she said, but she also seems to miss the salary Gilian earned as a schoolteacher.

On this ranch they found in eastern Montana, Gilian raises sheep and ponies, merely another form of patient management, he has said, and more predictable than seventh graders. He taught science. The weather in this part of the country, however, and over the rest of the world, too, as far as that goes, is undergoing changes everybody seems to have a theory about but nobody can fix. There has been no rain.

"Oh!" the boy cries in his sleep, and Gilian rests his head in the corner of his wingback chair, weary at the way Will seems to reflect their distress. These cries from him began the summer they moved here, when Gilian would carry the boy, thirteen months then, out to the tree row near the sheep pens and set him on a blanket under a lilac in bloom. Will would rise, still shaky on his feet, and reach for a rocky butte where the sky touched the horizon, as if he could take hold of the earth there, and then cry out as if he had. His cries in his sleep are identical to the ones he produced then.

Last week they were driving down a back road when Gilian had to slow and turn aside to miss the carcass of a raccoon, and Will, who was standing on the seat between the two of them, said, "Dad, do raccoons come from God?"

"Yes," Gilian said, tight-lipped at the parched look of drought on all sides. Then he slowed more, waiting for Will to make the connections that would move him to ask why God then let the raccoon die mangled along a roadside. But Will said, "They must come a long way." He calls moths "mops," grasshoppers "hoppergrassers," and hiccups "hickpups" and won't be corrected, as if his naming has added a dimension he can't give up.

Gilian shakes out the *Times* with enough noise to allow Anne to say "Let's talk." But she's absorbed in her novel with its candy-striped cover inset at the center with a globe. When he was in college, Gilian read novels, too, and was also interested in psychology—the more abnormal the better—and maybe it was reading of that kind, mostly imaginative, that had led him to think of this part of the state as largely unexplored, a no-man's-land, unlike the mountainy tracts that began at Billings and spilled west. He had worked in this area for several summers to earn spending money while he went to school, and came to love the aromatic task of making hay—the clatter of sickle knives polishing themselves silver on a thicket of stubble, the black-red domes of the badlands off to the east. So it was easy to decide with Anne to move here, once Will was born and the public schools had deteriorated so much that Gilian had an excuse to leave.

He lets the paper fall over his knees. The article he's been trying to read, one of a series on genetics, isn't up to the earlier batch. In one of those a researcher said there were clues that DNA carried encodings of memory, so that a child received not only language from both parents, but something of their pasts. And Gilian had thought, Why not? How else could children, almost from birth, have the facility they had to get parents to comply with their wishes? They must receive a complement of each of them through their entwined genes. Gilian closes his eyes just as Will cries out.

What is this struggle Will has with sleep? Gilian wonders, and starts to drift off himself. In the logic of half sleep he thinks that if Will has inherited a portion of their genes, then he, Gilian, has access to half of Will's. He tries to enter Will's state. He is crying at his mother's feet as she stands at the sink. He's kneeling in water on the floor, and suddenly the water is her. In a blur she's gone as he floats out the door with paper and hay from the broom—into a black dark Dad should protect him from.

There's the slam of the door that Dad makes when he's angry, and then a heat like light from the hot open stove. Blood flies like rubber over the snowbanks, and his mom's head comes bouncing up, a ball without a body, and lies there, her eyes on him in the snow. He tries to stop this, but she's saying something he has to hear, and when he moves closer, the bubbling bursts, and she's gone.

The swish and stomp of an ax. Dad's big boots below stumps. Blue night across the fields where stems of weeds stand thick and black. Dad's legs are close—the wheeze of his breathing like a windy day in the trees. Dad doesn't see that he's a stump among the ones a dad must chop. His ears close in on him in the way the wood is frozen into stacks inside the night. Dad won't see him without his ears—and now no hands or feet. Claws' stumps, like the chicken whose feet got frozen blue, so the ax went through its crop, *whump.* A *whee* like Dad's saw speeds up the wood, so that he's hurried toward the boots, past other stumps, to get him first. He tries to tell his dad, "No, he won't do it again, Dad. He'll obey!"

"Ahh!" the boy shrieks, and Gilian sits up. His hands look white. No way to hold the wind or cover up—no house with lights going on and off, or voices in the rooms of it at night.

"This has to stop," Gilian says.

Anne sighs and places her parted book over a knee. "Yes, it's such a relief once he's asleep."

"I mean . . ." Gilian stares down the hall at the barred door, as if Will might come crashing through it, and feels a draft from there over his ankles. He remembers how he pulled the door wide this morning and saw Will a ways off in a dazzle of snow, in his red snowsuit, bundled and wound with so many scarves he seemed barely able to move, his chapped and weather-reddened face turned toward Gilian. Behind the boy, hitched to his sled and setting the the end of its runners so deeply into the snow that he couldn't pull it any farther, was Will's heavy coaster wagon. And Gilian thought of how Will lately wasn't able to play unless he had something "hooked up," as he put it—a toy truck behind a car, a toy car behind a tractor—and the idea of this made Gilian shout, "What the hell are you up to! What are you *doing*! Don't you realize it's winter!"

His throat still feels clotted, as if he's spent the day in a rage, and he manages to get out "Oh!" He stands and feels he is rising through the layers of the night he has imagined, and understands that in some unsound way, in the isolation this life has forced on them, he has come to view Will as a threat. To him and Anne. Those bloody fantasies weren't Will's; they were his; they were out of control—harmful, he sees, and a feeling of constriction (as bad as being inside a four-year-old's skin) wraps and heats his face. He's been trying to supplant his own son. "Good God!" he cries.

Anne looks up at him, pink from the sunlight, and whispers, "Shh."

"He must think—" Gilian can't complete this without going all the way back, for Anne, to the beginning.

"Are you talking about Will?" she asks.

"No wonder the poor kid is afraid to death to go to sleep."

❄ Winter Insects

It's the mist, Les thought. It turned every form of light into an amorphous glow. Right now, just beyond his headlights, a silvery upheaval gathered in a swarm that assumed the shape of a tunnel (while sweeps of gold at the windshield's edge swung in and out of sight like curving lightning) and then was over the Wagoneer in a hoop. The lightning was really iced-over electrical wires, he knew, and for the past half hour he had used them to navigate by rather than the plowed banks lining the road—blinding behind the mist. But what this other was, he couldn't tell.

Beige columns probed the sky ahead, as if searchlights had been trained straight up, and then pale disks appeared out of a turbulence of light as a semitrailer burst past—impossible, it seemed, in the misty insubstantiality, if it weren't for the impact, like a pouring waterfall, at his side of the Wagoneer.

He had fought through fog from Lake Michigan on this blacktop before, but it had never been this bad. His eyes felt worn thin from the effort to see. Another swirl of light hooped the hood and windshield, and he brushed at his face, figuring it was a form of northern lights or something caused by the cold. *Not* the mist. It was below zero, with no wind. Then through the drizzling atmosphere he saw, at the edge of a village ahead, streetlights glow like yellow plates hung along a wire,

13

and heard his wife, Lynda, in the seat beside him, sigh, and then say, "Close to home."

He negotiated a hill, then a curve and a straight run, and swung off the blacktop onto their road—tawny gravel—and had to struggle in a different way to see; the banks here were as high as the roof of the Wagoneer. And then, as always on this road, as they continued to climb its grade toward the west, the mist was gone, that quick. They were in black night—a change so sudden he let up on the gas.

He glanced to see if Annie, his two-year-old, was asleep, since she'd been so quiet, and saw her kneeling in Lynda's lap, moving her mittened hands in a private orchestration. He'd been buying gifts for the two of them from the week before Christmas until now, January, and felt dead broke. He swerved to miss a pothole but hit it enough to feel the Wagoneer rock in a way that meant its shocks were shot. He'd spent too much on it, too, and it wasn't even the kind he wanted. Beneath its domestic exterior, he hoped to discover a C-J 5—the classic ragtop—but it was a dog.

In October, he had gone off the road and rolled their van. He had been alone, at three in the morning, driving back roads, as he did when he couldn't sleep, trying to memorize out-of-the-way woods, and had driven until sunrise, working at a six-pack on the seat beside him. Back on the route toward home, he had started screwing and unscrewing the floorshift, bored, and felt it come loose in his hand. He tried to get it back in place as he steered, startled, then heard the rumble of the tires on the shoulder. He could still picture, at the second the front wheel dug into sand, a growth of pines out the windshield go into a blurring change and trees appear in autumn colors under the sky (while he thought, What a way to go) and then an explosion like plates being smashed as he went blank, aware only of a scald through his nose. Then another impact took him back to where he'd started, staring down on a square of grass with every blade distinct, crushed and microscopic, under a sheet of glass. He found he could move and reached up to pull his stocking cap from a dome in the windshield where it had started through, and its yarns tore free with a stitching sound that set up a web of lines over his face. Then these took on the pattern of the shattered windshield and started running with itching warmth. Blood. He could taste it in a gouge across his tongue, which felt bit in two. But he had the sense to reach over—or *up*, actually— and shut off the ignition.

He had cracked a kneecap and cut his face in a way that left only one permanent scar, but sometimes, as he was driving, a sensation would travel across the pattern he'd felt on his face, and he had to brush at it like cobwebs.

He dimmed the lights, and their beams struck what seemed the end of the tunnel—a mound of snow where the road curved right—and he felt out of breath. The mound was at the foot of the lane that led up the hill to their house—or the lane used to, until the fellow who ran the plow had piled snow here, saying he could only maintain county roads on a winter like this, or the roads of people with kids in school.

Les let up on the gas for the curve and felt the knobby tires slip out of traction with a noise that unnerved him as much as the beginning skid. He pulled out of it quick, blinking and alert, and brushed a hand over his face.

"*Eeeee!*" Annie cried. She was rising in Lynda's lap, shoving at Lynda's hands around her waist, and then she jumped up and down and squealed, as if she had experienced the same tug in her stomach as he had from the skid. "Shh," Lynda whispered, to quiet her. He looked from the road to them, both their faces unearthly in the green light from the dash, and slowed even more.

Lynda said he drove too fast on the country roads ("Too

damn fast" is how she put it), and this was the last of them; it led to a farm of their nearest neighbor, Jake Nelson.

"She must not know where we are," he said, hearing an ominousness in his voice from not having used it for miles.

"No," Lynda said, and pressed her profile against Annie's coat in a way that reminded him— Of what? Since he'd crawled from the upended van, littered with glass, and kicked open its back door with his good leg, everything reminded him of something else.

"She was asleep," Lynda said. "But our rough road woke you, didn't it?"

"Ya," the girl said, with the intonation of one of the local Scandinavians—a flat longing.

"Now you've told her we're here," he said, concerned.

Annie wriggled forward to see out the window, getting free of Lynda's hands, and leaned on the dash. Then, in springy backsteps, she was against the seat between the two of them, biting a mitten. She hated the trail he'd blazed down the face of their hill. He had got stuck so many times in it, even with the Wagoneer, it scared her merely to be near it. Some nights she shouted, "No, no! Not!" and started crying. "Honey," Les would say, "it's only a hill." But he wondered how much she understood about his accident.

"She knows perfectly well where we are," Lynda said.

"Let's not argue." They had vowed not to with Annie present, because of the family arguments they had heard at her age. Since Annie was born, they had been traveling across the country, and when they needed money, Les took whatever job was handy until it was time to move on. They had decided to travel until they found the right place to live and meanwhile wanted to free Annie from every outside influence they could. They wanted to teach her their ideas or lead her to the thinkers they admired, rather than force her, at her age, to have to sift through the effects, familial and foreign, that the circumstances of everyday life brought up. They wouldn't let her watch TV.

"There's it!" Annie cried, and her mittened hand rose so close to his eyes he ducked.

He drove past the opening in the snowbank—he could see it out his window—that he had plowed wide on a downhill run at such a clip he had lodged the Wagoneer in the bank across the road. He always drove past the opening, nearer to Jake's, in order to get up speed for the angle he had to take in the tracks climbing the hill. Now he decided to try a longer run, for good measure, and then considered driving on to Jake's, to have the talk with him he'd been meaning to have for weeks. But what if Jake said no?

Les's present job was cutting wood. He sometimes took down trees for people who called, but the bulk of his business, as he thought of it, was selling firewood. Half the county was using wood-burning stoves, but not many who had invested in them had had the foresight to imagine how much work it was to keep one in wood. So Les felled diseased or dead hardwood and cut it into stove lengths and split it, if it had to be split, and hauled it to the aging hippies and well-to-do in Traverse County on a trailer hooked behind the Wagoneer. By investing in a chain saw and a sharpener and a maul, he became his own boss, and he had said to Annie, "To get ahead in the world, honey, all you have to do is work."

Lynda answered the phone, and they were pleased to be providing a necessary service. They were doing so well it seemed almost too good to Les, and business could only grow, to judge from the phone calls. Before the last heavy snow, he had thinned the woods around their house, which he had permission from their landlord to do, and he'd been meaning to ask Jake if he could move into his woods. But even if Jake said, "Go ahead, *sure*," it wouldn't be the same with somebody else involved. So Les was starting to scout out deadfall he was willing to beg for over the phone.

He put on the brakes, then backed into a Y-turn and heard Lynda produce a chattering sound to distract Annie.

"Chipmawk," Annie said, identifying the animal's call.

It was one of several he and Lynda imitated when they read to Annie from a book about wildlife—as relevant to learn about as human beings, they figured. At first they were embarrassed as mimics, but then a kind of contest began: Who could reproduce the calls with the most accuracy? They read from the book every night, lying on their stomachs in front of a gas heater in the living room of their barny summer house—the heater's flame reflected in the floorboards beside the book Annie held open under her outspread hand. The imitations were meant to acquaint Annie with the sounds she heard at night and so allay her fears, if she had any. In Les's case, they only heightened his awareness of local wildlife; his hearing was twice as acute since the accident.

Annie didn't seem bothered by owls or the way a yapping would rise from the stillness, and Les figured that at her age, with her sense of time, she felt she'd grown up in the woods. They had been here longer than anywhere—seven months, a quarter of her life. Before, they had lived in cities, but when he found that Lynda preferred the country and they heard that summer people were looking for house-sitters due to snowmobiles opening the backwoods to thieves, Les said that if this wasn't the right place, quite, it was about the right price.

"Why don't you try to *ease* up the hill?" Lynda asked.

"If I knew this was hitting on all six, or whatever, I would." He ended his turn by crunching the back bumper into the bank behind, which looked like a crimson mountain range in his rearview mirror, peaks smoking from their exhaust. He revved the Wagoneer. There were times when he sensed that its front wheels didn't fully engage, which would mean a problem of some sort with the locking hubs, and he'd got it stuck as often as the sedan they had had as a loaner before the insurance company settled up.

"Now if this would work," he said, engaging the shifting lever for the four-wheel drive.

"It must," Lynda said, "or we wouldn't have had the traction we've had at times."

He glanced at Annie, who was staring ahead with wide eyes, mittens over her ears, and decided not to respond.

He took off slowly, without the growl the tires went into when he was pressing the Wagoneer for as much momentum as he could achieve, and as they broke through the bank, rising into the air on a ridge beneath, he felt the same release he had when the van went into its airborne roll. But this was under control, now that they were free of the mist, on a snowy plain where firs and hardwoods formed a peninsula ahead—and that peninsula, near the hilltop, was his goal. "Hang on!" he warned at the same moment Annie cried out.

"What?" he asked, reluctant to give up his beginning. He was going at a good speed up the pair of tracks, bucking against the crust on both sides in a way that took constant correction (past a place where the holes of their footprints wandered in reminder of another attempt) and then climbing higher onto the plain that widened from the hill above—all of this lit by a moon he'd glimpsed in the rearview mirror, like one of those glowing yellow plates from the edge of town, full-blown and bloated, dogging them home.

When Annie cried again, her cry struck at the center of his nerves, intensifying for him the crystalline breadth and roll of the moonlit landscape.

"Wonderful!" he heard Lynda say above the engine, and in a flashing look between the two of them and his trail, he saw

Lynda draw Annie so firmly against her that the girl's snow cap slipped off, spilling gold hair. Lynda kissed Annie's forehead and called to him, "Isn't that wonderful?"

"What?" he asked. "She's cheering us on!"

"She said 'fireflies,' " Lynda shouted across at him, dodging her head around Annie to see him better.

"Fi-flies," Annie echoed, turning.

"Fireflies?" he asked. He looked farther up, then to his right, and saw that the headlights were illuminating a brilliance in the air—lit pinpoints. It wasn't snow, and possibly the moon partially lit what he saw. In bitter cold, like tonight's, the moisture in the air sometimes crystallized, and perhaps it was streaks of this kind of crystallization that had hooped the windshield. In the woods once, he had shut off his chain saw and sensed something other than the usual hollow throb of silence, and then he heard crackling in the air and saw crystals appear in front of his eyes and drift slowly down. The pinpoints could be similar crystals, he thought, and saw how their hesitating swoop and flicker had caused Annie to identify them as fireflies.

"Yes," he said, and wanted to explain the phenomenon by telling them about that afternoon in the woods—but for now he had this hill to negotiate.

"Look!" he said, however, as another swarm swam into visibility across the slope. "Isn't it remarkable!"

"No," Annie said, patting his arm in correction. "No, *fi*-flies." She put her face to his ear, as if she wanted to impress her words on him but wasn't sure how to carry the impulse through. He could feel her hurried breathing at his ear, and then she touched his face with a mitten. He turned and found her staring directly at him, her hair mussed, an entity entirely separate from him or Lynda, and understood that a man someday would take her up on her pleading look.

He swung back to his tracks, carrying the look along—the

unguarded appetite of a newborn for the world. But Annie wasn't a newborn! She was using language to describe an effect that she'd been the first to see. Her compact bulk beside him was like the center of the cargo of gifts in the backseat, and he realized he'd bought them for their effect on her.

"Oh!" he said, feeling he had to shelter her from his insight. "Look again, though. That's really—oops, this road—a kind of snow that looks like fireflies, isn't it? Fireflies couldn't— Just a second. Fireflies couldn't survive in the cold, could they? Those—" But he had arrived at the timberline and had to wrestle with the wheel as the tracks swung left into their lane. He got past this junction and went on up the hill—all of them quiet, expectant, staring ahead—and then pulled down the drifted drive, past piles of strewn wood, his trailer, the hulk of the van that had been towed here, and stopped the Wagoneer at the back door.

He shut off the engine and stared through trees so bare he could see constellations beyond them. He sometimes asked them to sit in silence with him outside the place before they went in, a practice of his since high school, on the nights when he returned from a date. That time alone in a car was separate from the past, the young woman he'd seen, and the future, whatever that might hold—an interim in which he could sit and listen to the engine tick as it cooled and feel himself fill with such satisfaction he didn't know why he couldn't step from a moment like this and sustain it the rest of his life.

He heard Lynda and Annie whispering, and then Annie swung toward him and began bumping his arm with the front of her coat, as she bumped his leg in the house when she wanted to be hugged. Wait, he started to say, but couldn't think what it was he planned to say, and then couldn't speak. He felt that something was moving near, as if out of the woods, and although he wanted to hurry into the heat of the house with them, he felt a layer of protection, like the mist, part in him and his senses take on the exalted focus they had had when he'd stared out the overturned van onto that patch of grass, like fernery under glass.

He remembered saying, "Fireflies couldn't survive in the cold, could they?," and tried to begin the story of that afternoon in the woods, when crystals had formed in front of his eyes, but the runaway thought arrived full force: he wanted Annie for his own. He took her in his arms, feeling her cling to him like a diminishment of himself, and could make out the scent of her skin mingled with the newness of the coat, another gift from him, and whispered, "You're right, honey. Fireflies."

He worked free of her, and as he unlatched his door and reached for the ignition (picturing his hand reach up toward that other), the keys took on the dazzle of those crystals she had pointed to in the headlights. He shoved open his door and stepped into the snow and felt afloat, hovering beside the overturned van while the red flashers of emergency vehicles strobed its sides, as if he had entered the moment that would always be sustained. And then he heard voices from the vehicle he stood beside, rising to him from a great distance, and they seemed to take on the tone of all of the women, young and old, that he had once believed he merely wanted to carry safely over the threshold home.

❀ Owen's Father

Recently, at the age of twenty-three, Owen Bierdeman had begun to feel the influence of his father, and it wasn't a pleasant one. His father was dead: he'd been dead for fifteen years. Throughout adolescence Owen had felt the need of anyone who loses a parent at an early age to fill in the outline of his father, to invent traits and features and predilections for him, and since it was difficult for Owen to remember his father and his mother could not or would not answer Owen's questions about him, Owen had fabricated and found he now faced a vast and spurious personality.

His mother was a presence Owen could rebel against or conciliate, hate or love, but every time he thought of his father, he felt he was beating against blackness. And when Owen moved to New York a year ago, freeing himself from his mother's territory, a change began. Working at the Overseas Press Club, where he edited teletype dispatches, or pacing his studio apartment, Owen began to sense that his attitudes and gestures and even a certain tone of voice had the feeling of being familiar. They were his father's. So Owen realized he had to separate what he had invented from the truth.

He imagined his father as regal, tall and imposing, and it wasn't until a month ago, in Chicago, when he spent the New

Year with his mother, that Owen discovered a chink. Most of his father's papers and personal effects had been disposed of after his death; Owen remembered his mother gathering these together (in grief or fury, he wasn't sure which, but in a rummaging hurry) and packing them up for the garbage man. So it was with surprise that Owen, sorting through photographs and report cards from his grammar school days, came across the passport. The man staring up from the inside cover was open-faced, with shy, wide eyes and a small chin. The only striking feature was the line of his eyebrows. His height was listed as five feet six, three inches less than Owen's, and this was his father. The passport was issued in 1953, the year of his death. Owen began trembling, slipped the passport into the pocket of his jacket, and took it back to New York.

He spent hours on a sleeping bag spread over his studio couch, studying the face of his father. The clipped square picture was like an opening that enabled Owen to enter areas of the past that had been sealed off, and as he traveled down corridors listening to voices, watching scenes replay themselves, he believed he was discovering the identity of his father, and this brought him closer to an understanding of himself.

In the earliest scene, Owen was sitting on a lawn. It was twilight. The grass was wet and moist and the air damp with sweetness. In front of him were flowers, their blossoms, at eye level, bright against the iron bars of a fence. Coming from behind, flowing over him in a reassuring stream, was the sound of adult voices. Owen was picking flowers and putting them in his mouth. Then there was a cry, and the voices stopped. His mother's face was in front of his, her lips moving in anger. She took the flowers from him and started slapping his hands. With another cry, she disappeared. First Owen heard a burst of laughter from behind and then sounds of movement in the flower bed. His mother rose from the flowers, straightened her dress, shook back her hair, and walked past Owen toward the voices. Then the stems in front of Owen parted, and his father's face, with that slash of eyebrow, appeared. There was a flower between his teeth.

On the days when Owen was left alone with his father—many times, if he wasn't mistaken—he remembered the two of them rolling a croquet ball back and forth across the wood floor and shoving toy trucks toward one another in startling crashes; he remembered his father walking on his hands down the hall, up the stairs to the second floor, and then doing a handspring at the top and landing on his feet. Once, Owen answered the doorbell and found his father on the porch, dressed like a bum; in a parrot's voice he asked Owen for a cracker.

Owen remembered a time when his father carried tables—end tables, the kitchen table, his library table—into the parlor, set them in a row, and covered them with rugs, forming a tunnel that ran from the door of the master bedroom, through the parlor, to the door of the dining room. Sitting in the middle of the tunnel, his father started telling a ghost story. In the semidarkness, Owen could see only his father's teeth and the whites of his eyes, and as his father got deeper into the story, Owen watched the whites of his eyes grow wider. When his father finished, there was a silence, and then he whispered, "Let's get the hell out of here," and Owen could still feel the chill that clung to his back as the two of them thundered on their hands and knees toward the lit door at the end of the tunnel.

And when they were alone together, his father would sit beside him on the couch, with an arm around Owen to steady the book that rested in Owen's lap. Owen had no memory of either of them speaking, though they must have, but he recalled a feeling of complicity, communicated to him by the agreeable sensation that traveled over his shoulders every time his father turned a page. On a Sunday morning when his parents were in bed and Owen was wandering from room to room in the silent house wondering what to do, he heard the metal clatter and thump of the Sunday paper dropping inside through the front-door slot. He took it to the couch, sat down, and started paging through the comic section. His mother came out of the bedroom, and he pointed out a word and asked her how to say it. She sat down beside him, and in a while realized he was reading.

"Gene," she called. "Eugene, come in here!" When Owen's father appeared in his bathrobe, she said, "He's reading the paper, for goodness' sake. He can read!"

His father shrugged and said, "I should hope so. He's almost five." His face was blank with a look of boredom. But when Owen's mother went toward the kitchen, obviously put out, his father winked and with a smile on his face pantomimed clapping his hands.

About a year after this, a change came over Owen's father that manifested itself then—and now, too, and as far into the future as anyone wanted to see—in his signature on the passport. The handwriting was flat and erratic, loosely formed, almost indecipherable, with none of the usual quirkiness or pretension of a signature. It looked like a reminder someone had scribbled to himself on a notepad. His father became silent and morose and lost so much weight gathers appeared in his trousers. Visitors and guests showed up at the house less frequently, and Owen's father, who was a professor of history, stopped doing imitations of his students, stopped reading aloud the answers from their tests, which even Owen recognized as humorous, and stopped working in his library, where he said he was "doing research."

Owen could remember the way his father had walked before, briskly, with long strides (this was why Owen had retained the image of a tall man, he decided), his hands plunged into his front pockets instead of swinging loose, as though their movement could impede his momentum, which gave him a look of being off balance and hurrying forward to prevent a fall. Now he wandered aimlessly around the house, as Owen did on Sundays, his thin hands at his sides, looking naked, his eyes expressionless.

Owen remembered waking at strange hours and blinking against the overhead light in his bedroom. His father would be seated in a chair beside the bed, playing his guitar and staring at Owen as he sang. He sang several songs each night, but there were two he always sang: one was the story of a man hanged from a gallows tree, which was adapted, Owen later discovered, from a poem by Robert Burns, and the other was about bells in different cities. Owen could remember only one of the verses, but he could still hear the tone of his father's voice as he sang

> *All will be well if—if—if—*
> *Say the green bells of Cardiff.*

When his father finished, he rose without a word and switched off the light, and all Owen could see was a silhouette against the lighted doorway. The silhouette grew larger, became a shadow that engulfed Owen, and then Owen felt a kiss on his lips. The shadow's breath was sweet and cidery, and its smell, as Owen later learned, was from beer. Then the shadow drew away, and a silhouette, enlarged by a guitar, went toward the doorway and for a second, as it was struck by the hall light, changed into Owen's father. He disappeared, his footsteps going down the carpeted stairs and then resounding in the hardwood foyer. Then the lighted doorway Owen was staring at went black.

One night Owen awoke to blackness (trees shielding the window kept his room as dark as a closet) and heard voices downstairs. There was an urgent quality to them, and they sounded like the voices of strangers. He could imagine few reasons for strangers being in the house at that hour, none of them good, and as he continued to listen, his eyes moving as if sight were necessary to hearing, he realized the voices didn't belong to strangers; they were the voices of his father and mother, pitched in a way he'd never heard them before. He went to the stairwell and heard the voices coming from the other end of the house, not their bedroom, as he'd thought, but couldn't make out what they were saying.

He went down the stairs, tiptoed across the hardwood foyer, and stepped into the parlor. The dining room ahead was dark, but the tops and edges of furniture glowed, and a pair of glass candlesticks cast rainbow-tinted streaks across the table. The light came from the kitchen. His parents were arguing there. Owen had heard them argue before, and it shamed him, and he would have gone back upstairs if it hadn't been for the quality of their voices; they seemed to be defending themselves against a third person.

"—not normal," his mother was saying. "A normal person wouldn't act like this."

"What's normal?"

"A normal person would accept it."

"I did, once."

"This is something I just remembered."

"Remembered! How many more are you going to remember at how many more opportune times?"

"Look at your own past. Do you like what you see?"

"I've been truthful."

"And so have I, now."

"Now! When will 'now' stop?"

"Don't you see what you're doing?"

"Do you?"

There was a sound of running footsteps, a clattering, and Owen started to tremble.

"Is this what you want?"

When cries came from his mother, Owen knew somebody else was in the kitchen and ran through the door. His mother was just inside it, standing against the table, her back to him, and his father stood at the other end of the room, beside the refrigerator. He had a butcher knife in his hand.

"What are you doing down here?" his father asked.

"Now look what you've done," his mother said. "Aren't you proud of yourself?"

"Owen, get upstairs!"

Owen ran across the room, took hold of his father's bathrobe, and started kicking his legs and screaming. His mother pulled Owen away, wrestled and dragged him upstairs, got him into his bedroom, and gave him the most prolonged and painful spanking he'd ever had, and it wasn't until after she left his room and locked the door that the details of the scene in the kitchen registered. Owen realized his father wasn't threatening his mother with the knife. He held it against his own chest.

That weekend, the three of them drove in their new car to the cabin at Lake Geneva. No one spoke on the way up. Gray sky and the whine of tires on pavement like tenuous ribbons that held them intact. Instead of standing on the ridge in the center of the car and leaning his elbows on the front seat, as he usually did, so he could see the passing countryside, Owen sat alone in the back, watching telephone wires swoop up in a rhythm as regular as his breath and then drop from sight, only to start climbing until a treetop, exploding into view, destroyed the sequence. In the resort town, Owen's father went into a grocery store and came out with supplies. He put them in the backseat with Owen, and when they got to the cabin, they discovered that a dead limb had blown from a tree and broken out a window. Owen's father predicted the fishing equipment and furniture would be gone, but nothing had been touched. Then he predicted it would rain.

It was a cold fall day, evening was coming on, and since there was no hope of getting the window repaired until the next day, Owen's mother hung bath towels over it. They had owned the cabin for a year and had only used it that summer. Owen's father had to clean beer cans and trash out of the firebox of the stove before he could light it—a low oil burner that sat in the main room of the cabin. A small bedroom led off the main room, a sleeping porch off the bedroom, and there was a kitchen with enough space for dining. As soon as dinner was over, they went to bed, Owen on a couch next to the stove, his parents in the bedroom.

What followed was fragmented in Owen's mind. He awoke outside on the grass, on his stomach, his throat choked with a sewery smell, and something was on top of him, crushing him, lifting away, then crushing him again, and from a great height a voice he'd never heard was repeating, "Answer me. Answer me." Owen took a deep breath, and when he released it, he realized he was screaming. He felt he'd drawn fire into his lungs. He started coughing, and the coughing hurt worse. Then he was vomiting, and hands lifted him by his ribs and held him away from the grass.

Then he was in somebody's arms; he felt the person striding, heard the person murmuring something, and then was sitting on the cabin steps beside his mother. She took him in her arms and said, "Thank God," and at the sight of her tears Owen was sure his father was to blame for whatever had happened. The proof of this was that his father was gone. He pulled away from his mother and saw, against a tree a few steps away, his father staring at them with a fear Owen had never seen in him before.

If anybody was to blame for the incident, it was the person who installed the oil burner. Owen's father cursed himself for not checking its smokestack. Instead of rising above the roof, as it should have, the pipe stopped below the eaves, where there was no air circulation, and the gases from burning, he said, backed into the cabin. He had awakened, suffocating, in the middle of the night, had carried Owen outside, carried out his wife, who revived in the air, and for longer than he wanted to think about, he said, he gave Owen artificial respiration.

"But the act of providence that broke those windows is what saved your life," his father said. "Not me. That and your mother's instincts. Any other woman would have covered that window with something solid."

The half-moons at the base of Owen's fingernails were cherry red, and he and his parents had headaches the rest of the weekend. They didn't feel well enough to eat. But Owen remembered those two days as his happiest. Though his father's humor didn't really return, he became teasing and effusive in a new way, and a feeling of solidarity grew between them; they were content to sit in the cabin and entertain one another. Owen's father played the guitar and sang. His mother told about a trip she took to San Francisco when she was a girl, after her parents died (Owen's father's parents weren't living, either), that Owen had never heard about. They started *Anna Karenina* together, each reading a chapter aloud. With his parents sitting on either side of him, prompting him when he came to a difficult word, Owen felt himself mature with each sentence. "When you come to one of those long, impossible names," his father said, "rattle it off fast, like I do, so everybody figures you know what you're up to."

On the last evening at the cabin, they walked along the shore of Lake Geneva, their hands linked, and looked at the cabins and houses, the summer mansions, and the docks where dozens of boats, drawn out of the water for winter, were hanging under curved roofs of corrugated tin, swinging with a wind in the moonlight. The wind rocked the branches of the trees above, and leaves scattered over them like the rain Owen's father had predicted.

Far out on the lake, a rowboat stood alone on the water, and against the channel of moonlight on the lake they could see the silhouette of a single man in the boat, but the thin fishing rod, which from the position of his hands he apparently held, was invisible. The wind carried the sound of the man's voice to them, and they heard him singing to himself in a gentle bass. "He must be scared out there," Owen's father said. "That's why he's singing. He's trying to scare off what he's scared of." Then he added in a lighter voice, "Or the past," and Owen felt his mother's hand tense.

By the time they drove home, the solidarity that had begun was gone. Owen's father woke him again at night, he drank more, and many mornings there was no breakfast for Owen. He was afraid to disturb his mother, who seemed ill and kept to her bed, so he either poured himself some breakfast food and ate alone or went to school without. A few weeks later, Owen's father left for Lake Geneva, saying he had to fix the stove before winter. He was supposed to be gone for the weekend, so Owen was surprised to see him hurry through the front door the next morning and into the master bedroom. Owen went back to the table and continued his breakfast of cold cereal and milk.

His father walked into the kitchen with his overcoat on and sat across from Owen, hands in his pockets, his face drawn, unable to look at Owen. "Did your mother put you to bed last night?" he asked.

"Yes."

"Did you fall asleep right away?"

"I couldn't."

"Did you hear anybody come or go in the house?"

"Is something wrong?"

"Of course not. Did you hear anybody?"

"No."

"You're sure?"

"Isn't Mom here?"

"Of course she's here! What's the matter with you?"

"Is something wrong out at the lake?"

"Where do you get the idea that something always has to be wrong!"

His father got up and left the table.

That week, the week of Thanksgiving, Owen's father didn't have classes at the university and stayed home. His mother was in bed, sick with a cold, his father said, and "strep throat, strep throat." His father lifted his chin and made raking motions with his fingers down his neck. That was practically all his father said that weekend. The rest of the time he wandered around in a bathrobe, his face darkening with the beard he didn't bother to shave, and performed only the tasks he had to—washing dishes, fixing Owen's meals, and waiting on his wife.

When Owen's vacation began, two days later, there was such an unsettled feeling in the house, he stayed in his own bedroom. He would feel eyes on him and look up from his game of solitaire or the book he was reading and find his father in the doorway in his bathrobe.

"What?" Owen would ask, but his father would merely shake his head and walk off. If Owen went downstairs, his father trailed after him like a younger brother, following him everywhere, and once Owen was back in his room, it would only be a while before he felt eyes on him and knew his father was in the doorway. Once, in response to Owen's question, his father said, "Who am I?"

"What?"

"Who am I?"

"You."

"Who's that?"

"My dad."

"Good."

On Thanskgiving, Owen came down for dinner prepared by the atmosphere at school. The teachers said Thanksgiving was one of the few holidays every family in America celebrated, and the students produced cutouts of turkeys and pumpkins and cornucopias overflowing with food—Owen carried some of these under his shirt as a surprise. His parents weren't in the dining room; it was empty, and the table wasn't set. Drawn by the smell of cooking, Owen went into the kitchen. His father had dinner—macaroni and cheese—dished out on paper plates. Owen's mother wasn't there.

His father saw his expression and said, "I know. I'm sorry. We'll make up for it next year."

Owen sat and stared at his plate.

"I even checked the mailbox," his father said. "No drumsticks there. I guess nobody loves us, huh?"

The edges of Owen's plate melted, and he turned and took hold of the back of his chair.

"Oh, Owen, what's the matter? Is it the matter with you or the matter with me?"

"I want Thanksgiving!"

"Is that it?" his father said. "Okay!"

His father got out of his chair and squatted, making wings of his arms, and began to waddle around the kitchen, gobbling like a turkey. In spite of his tears, Owen started laughing, in painful seizures at first, and then he realized it was the first time in months his father had done anything so foolish. His father's face turned crimson, and his eyes, goggling ahead, started to bulge, but he continued to waddle around the table, gobbling in a growing voice until there was a sudden catch in Owen; he was afraid his father wouldn't stop. He got out of his chair and backed toward the door. The gobbling kept up, and then his father fell on the floor and covered his face with his hands. Owen turned and ran through the house and up the stairs, and the chill that pursued him now, unlike the one that clung to him when he escaped from that improvised tunnel, had a human shape.

Owen awoke from a restless sleep. Had there been a dream? His body was coated with sweat. The room was black, impenetrable, but after lying awake, he was sure, from the texture of the air as much as anything, that he wasn't alone. "Dad?" he said. There was no response. "Dad?" He thought he heard the sound of breathing. "Dad?" He held his breath to listen, but his ears filled with the growing beat of his own heart. Without the aid of sight, it was impossible to locate the sound he heard, and its source seemed to change. It sounded as if somebody was breathing above him, then breathing beside his right ear, and then standing in the doorway, breathing heavily there.

Owen sat up, or made the muscular equivalents that should result in sitting, and felt he was rising out of his body, as infinite as the dark. If he was still lying in bed, then this person rising from him was someone he didn't know who encompassed the room and responded to the breathing as if the breathing came from that person's center. Then, in a jarring reversal, Owen felt miniature and solid, an eight-year-old in a bed. He'd heard the springs in his dressing chair adjust to somebody's weight.

"*Dad?*"

"Don't be afraid. I didn't want to wake you."

"What's wrong?"

"Nothing."

"You sound funny."

"I wanted to sit with you. Did I frighten you?"

"No," Owen said, afraid to admit the truth.

"I'm sorry about that scene in the kitchen. I got carried away, huh?"

Was it the night of the knife? Owen lay unmoving, trying to identify the quality in his father's voice.

"Maybe it's better you woke. I can say out loud what I was thinking." His father felt along the covers until he found Owen's hand, and Owen nearly jerked it away; his father's hand felt rinsed in ice water. "I came to say good-bye."

"Where are you going?"

"Up to the cabin."

"Can I come?" Owen didn't want to, but felt that this was what his father wanted him to say.

"No. I scare you to death. You're trembling right now." He drew his hand away.

Now Owen was afraid he'd hurt his father's feelings. "I do want to go. I'll go with you."

"Maybe later we'll take a trip. Would you like that?"

"Yes."

"I might even take you out of school. What do you think of that?"

"I like school."

There was a long pause, and in the silence Owen felt a shift in the atmosphere; it was as if the third person he'd sensed in the kitchen had entered the room.

"I could teach you," his father said, and the tone of his voice, confirming the altered state of the room, seemed to allow the third person to start breathing. "If you didn't like that, we could try a tutor."

"What's a tutor?"

"Like me. He'd go wherever we went and teach whatever you wanted to learn, whenever you wanted to."

"Where would we go?"

"I don't know. Out of state. Maybe out of them all."

"To another country?"

"Maybe." Then there was a change in his voice that made Owen feel a light had been switched on. "But we can talk about that later. Now I want to go up to the cabin for a few days and fix that stove I never fixed and think things through. Your mother has an inkling I'm going but doesn't know for sure when, and I'm not going to bother to wake her, so in the morning tell her I left, okay? Say there's a note for her on the buffet. And— You have to sleep. Are you asleep?"

"No."

"Good." There was an inconclusive silence. "Don't forget to mention the note."

"No."

Owen heard a creak of springs as his father leaned and felt over the covers for his hand. He took it in his. "I'm going now."

Owen could feel his indecision and suppressed emotion— a reluctance, almost a plea—and in the silence the dark air started to vibrate. Then the quality of it came to Owen, and he said, "Sing a song before you go."

The edge of the mattress sank under his father's arms, tilting Owen toward him, there was the thump of his knees hitting the floor, and Owen could smell his father's hair.

"Oh, Owen, I'm so sorry!"

Owen felt that the bed was dissolving in the darkness, and

his fear must have been communicated through his hand. His father released it and stood, and as he stood, the room returned to its former state; a third person was in it.

His father's voice came from a changed height: "I'm going."

"When will you be back?"

"Oh . . ."

"I miss you already."

"I miss you."

The darkness established a pact of understanding, unspoken, in which Owen felt endangered.

"Good-bye," his father said.

"Do you have to go?"

"Yes."

His footsteps descended the carpeted stairs, started across the hardwood foyer, and then hesitated. The third person left the room. The footsteps, moving more rapidly, went on across the foyer to the front door: the knob turning, the door swinging in, a key being inserted, footsteps, the door pulled to, the snick of the latch, the key withdrawn. Silence. The silence gathered in Owen's room and rested above him, a probing presence with a question left unanswered.

"Dad?" Owen asked.

Owen tossed aside the passport, got out of his sleeping bag, and went to the window. It was Saturday night. His apartment was a story up, and through the bars of the fire-escape landing he watched the weekend crowd—girls with streaming hair in shirts and jeans, bearded men, men in suits, tourist couples, teenagers—move in a press down Thompson. A Puerto Rican delivery boy, holding a box of pizza aloft, traveling twice as fast as the crowd, threaded his way through it in a movement like a dance and passed beneath Owen's window whistling, borne on his way by the thought of dinner later with others, Owen imagined. He turned to his room.

Dust was everywhere, and two charred logs, left in the fireplace by the previous resident, lay like fixtures. The only furniture besides the studio couch, a chair with a wired leg, was draped with newspapers. Just the idea of cleaning up, the acknowledgment of disorder, fatigued Owen. He eased his weight onto the edge of the windowsill.

The rest of the story was simple. When he awoke that night after his father left, he lay in bed trying to decipher the visit, and then, realizing it might be in his power to uncover the reason for his father's behavior, he got out of bed and went down the steps, silent, past the master bedroom, to the buffet, where a lamp burned. His father's note was beside it, weighted with a book of matches. Owen slipped the note under the elastic belt of his pajama bottoms and started toward the stairs.

His mother stood at the end of the hall.

"What are you doing down here?"

"Looking for Dad."

"At three in the morning?" Her hair was haloed by light from the bedroom, and Owen couldn't see her features.

"I got scared. I had a bad dream."

"You were looking for him in the living room?"

"I saw the light."

"You know perfectly well your father is in bed."

"No, he isn't."

"What?"

"No, he isn't."

"Are you contradicting me?"

"He went to the cabin. He came and told me he was going there. He said I was supposed to tell you."

She reached and lifted a strand of hair from her forehead, and her voice became reflective. "Then he went."

Owen nodded.

"When was this?"

"I don't know. It was dark."

"Did he say anything else?"

"No."

"He didn't leave a message for me?"

"He said he had to fix the stove and think awhile."

She turned, her negligee billowing, went to a panel of switches on the wall, and turned on the light to the stairs. "All right. Go to bed."

Owen walked past her, hearing the paper crackle in his pajamas, and started up the steps. The note slipped from the belt and started working down a pajama leg. He slowed, lifting the leg woodenly because the cuffs of his pajamas didn't fit tight around his ankles.

"Owen!"

He stopped, unable to see her from where he stood, unsure whether she could see him, and felt his heartbeat pick up. "Yes."

"If your father said good-bye, how does it happen you were downstairs looking for him?"

Finally, pawing past the shades of his lying, he said, "I wasn't sure he left yet. I fell asleep for a while and wanted to tell him something before he left."

"What did you want to tell him?"

"To see if he could find some pinecones for my science class."

He'd forgot about the dream he'd mentioned. There was an extended silence. "All right," his mother said. "Go to bed. I'll turn out the light."

He did not go to bed. When the door of the master bedroom closed and there was silence, he went to the dresser, found by touch a penlight and school notebook, and went into his closet and shut the door. He took out the note and, shining the penlight on it, read it through. Then, for the next hour or so, he sat in the closet and committed it to memory. If a word was unfamiliar, he made up a pronunciation and copied it down in his notebook, to have the correct spelling. When he opened the closet door, morning lay blue over his window. He chewed up the note and swallowed it and then lay under the covers, trying to relate the message to the recent attitudes of his parents.

It's not all histrionics, as you seem to think. It's actually that bad. You can blame it on my childness maybe—I do—but that still doesn't help. I need to be alone, so I've gone to the cabin. Then I think Europe for a while, and then we'll see. It must be Europe. Living apart and being this close doesn't work, as I've aptly, as I've aptly demonstrated. There's one thing I want you to think over. If it's Europe, can Owen come with me? No, *please*, before you say no, think about it.

It cleared up little of the mystery, and there it stayed. Three days later, Owen's father was dead. His mother didn't want Owen to attend the funeral, there weren't close relatives to console him or explain, and he didn't discover any details of the death, other than its cause, until he was in college and learned that back issues of newspapers were recorded on microfilm. He copied down the article that he still carried with him.

AREA PROFESSOR FOUND DEAD IN LAKE GENEVA CABIN

Dr. Eugene T. Bierdeman, associate professor of history at the University of Chicago, was found dead about 11:00 A.M. today in his summer cabin at Lake Geneva in Walworth County, Wisconsin, apparently the victim of carbon monoxide fumes from an oil heater, according to the Walworth County sheriff's office.

Dr. Bierdeman was 39 and resided on Bonnie Brae Lane in Clarendon Hills. He had been an instructor for seven years at the University of Chicago, the institution from which he obtained his doctorate in 1951. His area of specialty was the 15th century.

His immediate superior, Dr. Warren Schilling, said today to reporters, "We are shocked and grieved to learn of this tragedy. Gene Bierdeman was not only an exemplary teacher but a friend to us all. He was emulated by his colleagues and loved by his students."

Discovery of the body was made by Chief Deputy Wayne Burdette of the Walworth County sheriff's office, who went to the cabin at the request of Bierdeman's wife to find out why Bierdeman had not returned home or appeared to teach his classes this morning.

According to Chief Deputy Burdette, the oil heater had not been functioning properly, he learned from Mrs. Bierdeman, and Bierdeman had made the trip to the three-room cabin in Linn Township to repair it over the weekend. Burdette said that the stack of the vent pipe was not tall enough to permit proper venting.

Bierdeman had removed the stack, apparently to add to it two additional sections of pipe that were found in the vicinity, but had proceeded no further, possibly because of the approach of darkness, speculated Burdette. Burdette said that Bierdeman apparently assumed that it would now be safe to operate the burner.

But Burdette said that the vent pipe from the heater itself let through the side wall of the cabin at the same level as the heater, and authorities are speculating that the wind, which shifted to the south Saturday night, prevented the exhaust fumes from escaping from the pipe and forced them back into the cabin.

An alarm clock, set for 7:00 P.M., was found in the cabin, and it is believed, from the condition of the body when it was discovered, that Bierdeman died sometime Friday night and that death can be attributed to asphyxiation by carbon monoxide fumes.

Inquest into the death has been set for 3:00 P.M. Tuesday in the Walworth County coroner's office.

Dr. Bierdeman is survived by his wife, Elizabeth, and a son, Owen.

"So," Owen said, and was startled to hear his voice, as rusty as an old man's. He went to the studio couch, picked up the passport, folded back its cover, and stared at the picture, trying to arrange the shifting scenes containing his father, but too much was unresolved, there were too many contradictions, too much had happened in between—there was no *hope*, Owen nearly said aloud, and felt his bones ache.

He went into the bathroom with the passport and held his head under the water faucet. He combed back his wet hair and, staring into the mirror, held the passport beside his face and compared it to the picture. Though the resemblance wasn't that striking, the faces over the months had become identical to him, and now he was so arrested by their similarity that he felt himself fill with the exhilaration he felt when he saw a woman he wanted; his heartbeat picked up, and his stomach dropped as it did on an elevator, while the objects in his vision, as if assuming lives of their own, lifted from their surroundings and came sailing into focus. The third person he'd sensed in the room was at his side, and he was sure it would only be a matter of time before he would be freed from the past, as he'd come to convince himself his father had been freed, by the suicide he felt it was necessary for him to commit.

❦ Summer Storms

Now I understand why summer can surprise us more than other seasons. It might begin in this way: out of the stillness of a humid afternoon, in the midst of which you sit with a gnat whining at your ear in enhancement of your solitude, you hear a rending like a tree splitting down its middle and then an explosion worse than a crate of dynamite going off. After you recover and begin a tour of the house to close the windows, the rain starts, or the hail, or a combination of them, and you begin to wonder, as you test your inner fear of a tornado, why it is that you've never trained your family to take a quick route to the safest part of the basement when they feel a trembling through the house like an overloaded locomotive approaching.

What makes summer storms so pernicious is the resistance in our nature to admit them. We acknowledge the naturalness of storms in the spring, yes, when rain on the roof can assume the sound of a waterfall; or in the winter, with a howling wind accompanying drifting snow; or even in the fall, when heavy-bodied rain tears off the last of the leaves and pastes them over spearing stubble. But summer is the season we're to be let off, to be free of this, as we expect to be freed from texts and tests and every onerous chore, after the ingrained conditioning of years in school. So summer storms set us outside our expectations and isolate us physically, since we don't take the precautions we do during other seasons, but expect to take the summer off as recklessly as—well, that storm on its way.

It was a long, dry summer, the same season in which I watched twin tornadoes set down from a black-green sky and spin themselves out without harm. I was working in an outer shed on the ranch where we live when I realized that I was enveloped in utter silence. Then, in the distance, I heard the rumble of that overloaded locomotive approaching. I thought of my family in the house and went for the door of the shed and opened it against a sound like rifle fire.

Hailstones the size of marbles, then golf balls, were ricocheting off everything in sight. A few hit my hand at the half-open door. I pulled it shut, and out a pair of my high windows, which I had newly installed that summer but had yet to equip with locks, I saw the anvil-shaped cloud, and then, with a sudden drop in pressure I could feel inside my ears, all four windows sprang wide, wobbling on their hinges, and pages of a handwritten manuscript started climbing out the closest opening in a chattering stream.

I grabbed at the pages, batting a few down, but only stirred things up worse, and now the shed was shaking, and everything loose was springing toward the windows in a rattling swirl past my face. The hail had forced the door inward, I saw, and went for it, but so much ice had built up I couldn't get it closed, and suddenly a fresh wash of rain, mixed with hail, sprang from the exact direction necessary to enter the door, and a carpet I'd lugged all the way from New York rumpled up and then swung across my legs with a new blast of wind. I was soaked and dripping in seconds. "And it's summer!" I almost cried, as if my statement could bring the incongruity of all this to a stop.

After the small tornado, I gathered from our fields as much of the manuscript as I could get my hands on, and then my daughter and my niece, who was visiting, began to make wider rounds. Over a hundred pages were lost, but by the time the two of them had covered a radius of eighty or more acres, alert to the glint of pages, the task of reconstructing the manuscript started to seem less hopeless. Each sheet had to be spread out to dry, and some were battered so badly it took tape to reassemble them, but I had written in pencil, not ink; nearly everything was legible. And as I began to recover more pages, or shreds of them over the summer, I began to feel that nearly nothing was irrevocable.

I have been in summer storms as bad, when a house trembled above the corner of the basement where my family huddled, praying; when a waterspout developed off a beach on Lake Michigan, so distant over the water that a group of us blithely went on with our picnic, only to see it suddenly swerve inland, tilting and swaying at its top. It started up the beach as all of us scattered, everything from the tables swooping up, and soon became so overweighted with sand it gave out with a sound like the contents of a swimming pool falling five stories.

But the glory of summer storms is their diversity: heat lightning traveling like networks of nerves through evening clouds; the hazy pinpricking rains of the Pacific Northwest; bronze-tinged banks of smog over L.A., and the dangerous wind-driven sea south of Catalina Island as the smog blows off; storms of cottonwood pollen along inland rivers, called summer snow by French voyageurs, and the actual startling August snows of the upper Rockies; firestorms in forests darkening a dozen states with pine-sweet smoke; sleet ticking against derricks and oil drums in Manitoba; the magnetic storm of northern lights over the upper latitudes, igniting the dome of heaven from the north all the way overhead to the south with pulsing currents of gold and pastels; a cloudburst descending from a lime green sky on the Texas Gulf—a gullywasher in which torn-off leaves skate down a clay brown current laced with bubbling foam; the windstorms, called "monsoons" by local Arizonans, that assault the desert in late July and pile up such towering clouds of dusty silica that the dimmed sun shimmers like a coppery star; the tropical rains of south Florida that come like clockwork, every day near noon, falling in dollops of drops large as quarters, and then rise in a steamy humidity to fall at the same hour the next day; those atmospheric inversions over Chicago and the stilled, muffled air that tastes of ozone; the rains that transform New York into an equatorial capital in August, when even the potted ferns outside hotels appear to wilt in the sticky texture and all of the best psychiatrists, even those who served residencies in Vietnam, take off for Europe or the Cape.

And there is the summer storm that most of us have experienced at least once. You rent a house or cabin at the ocean or on a lake or cape or bayou or bay and arrive with the whole family, one of the few opportunities you'll have to enjoy summer together. The first night, as you lie in bed trying to sleep, you become aware of a sound like squirrels scrabbling on the roof. Rain.

You fall asleep to the sound and wake to blue light and go to the window; it hasn't let up. It's a gentle summer rain, such a dallying drizzle you can scarcely make out the drops, the kind of rain you look forward to for your lawn's sake—but not here. The children are arguing. You get out the picture puzzles in their broken and taped boxes, reproduced in the garish colors of the forties, pull an old murder mystery from a bookshelf, and crawl back into bed to wait this out.

It doesn't let up. At the grocery or general store the locals are exultant; this will be great for the crops, they crow. Such a *gentle* summer rain, they say. Back at the rented place, your

47

spouse complains that you're making the drinks too stiff and having one after the other. The children won't stop arguing. You suggest that they run out and play in the rain, splash in puddles, and at their looks you realize how much they've aged. Then you remember that it's in the spring, anyway, when puddles attract them; by the summer they want the real thing. They're *bored*, they say, and you wonder why it is that when you talked for weeks about this vacation, you found it necessary, like a bland travel poster, to emphasize the sun so much.

You go to the window once more and experience the perverse joy of the natives; there is no sign of this letting up, and the grass and leaves everywhere look bejeweled with billions of drops. To break up the worst of the children's fights you take down a chess set and call a son to you at the card table you've set up. The rain continues overhead until the last day of your rental.

Out on the beach, finally in the sun, you're grudgingly grateful at least for this, and you realize that the time has been instructive. You'll have to stop drinking. Your wife, you've learned, wants a new car, since it's largely fallen to her to transport the children everywhere; and your youngest son, about whom you've harbored a secret fear of his being slow, is more than your equal at chess, and has perhaps always only needed your encouragement. And the daughter you thought was becoming a slugabed actually gets up as early as always but now spends an hour each morning at the reading you've recommended, and then another hour at the mirror. Of all of the children, she is the one who has matured the most—suddenly a young woman—and you might have missed this, along with the way she's beginning to take on your mannerisms and characteristics, if it hadn't been for this season of enforced closeness caused by the gentlest of summer rains.

But the definitive storms occur in isolation, like the one that struck when I was thirteen, at the most susceptible age. I was working that summer on a ranch near the Montana border, twenty miles from the nearest town, riding a horse every day, helping with the livestock and haying, and I was interested in a girl—the daughter of the nearest neighbor, several miles out of the river valley where the ranch lay, across coulee-intersected hills. Siobhan, I'll call her. Her father, a Skoal-dipping cowboy, was known for his skill with the fiddle and his temper, and Siobhan was said to have inherited everything from him but his musical talent. I rode with the family in their Chevrolet every Sunday to church, a forty-mile drive, and during that ride the family divisions, and my separation from them all, became apparent.

Siobhan's father and mother perched in the front, at opposite sides of the seat, her father at the wheel in his black cowboy hat, and never talked. Siobhan had a brother my age, and the three of us shared the backseat; if I didn't sit beside him, he got angry, and if I sat beside Siobhan, with her in the middle, the constant silent fight between them nearly undid me. That he would elbow her! If I sat in the middle, in torment at her nearness, speechless, their battle seemed to occupy my lap, and if my leg or hand or shoulder touched Siobhan, her freckled face flamed to the roots of her coal-black hair, and she let me have it so hard with an elbow I doubled over. She was fifteen.

She was celebrating her birthday that summer and invited me to the party, which I thought meant *me*; that is, I figured I was her date. But the wife of the rancher I worked for said, "If I know Siobhan, she's invited every man and boy who can stand upright from here to Miles City and all the way down to Bismarck and back."

On the day of her party a wind started up, the sort of summer wind that can plague the western plains like a sirocco, and I began dressing two hours early. I'd bought a new pair of cowboy boots from a mail-order catalog, a cowboy shirt, buckskin riding gloves, and one of those basket-weave cowboy hats, spray-painted white, that were the style then. I saddled up Lady, an aging mare who was mine to ride that summer, and saw from her skittishness that the weather was getting worse. Rapid black clouds were flaring so thickly across the sky, it was turning dark. By the time I led Lady to the ranch house it seemed we were in the midst of an eclipse.

"Should I go?" I asked the rancher, who had turned on the pole light and stepped outside.

"Why wouldn't you?" he asked in the cheery, encouraging way he had of dealing with everything, including nature.

"It's so dark—" I looked around as if to indicate the storm.

"Lady knows the way."

His wife came to the screen door, in yellow kitchen light that appeared to contain warmth, and said, "You wouldn't want Siobhan to think you aren't man enough to ride a few miles to see her on her birthday, would you?"

The rancher helped me mount; I couldn't reach the stirrups and was usually able to leap high enough to crawl on board but found I couldn't in my squeaky new regalia.

"Go to the spring and then take the trail east," he said. "It hits at their gate. Snug that gate up good."

He had stepped back as he spoke, and I could barely see his body below his hat brim. I swung Lady around on a road I could just see (it was that dark) and was about to turn back when I saw the rancher's wife still at the door. I gave up trying to make out the road and kept Lady true to course by the sound of her hooves on packed ground. And when I was off the road? In my hesitation of thought Lady pivoted and headed for home.

We were beyond the stand of protective trees that sheltered the house, and with the wind tearing at my hat and clothes, it wasn't easy to slow her. She was headstrong if she sensed you didn't have the upper hand—"muley," the rancher called her— "ridden by too many children," and it took some doing to turn her back.

The spring was a half mile off, and by the time we got there I was tired of trying to hold my hat on and keep her headed right. As I looked up the darkened valley, she found the spring, from the way her head went down, nearly jerking the reins from my gloved hands, and I let her drink. The spring was in the crevice of a valley extending to the hilltops, and the trail, I knew from herding cows, ambled along the topside of the valley. I started her up, and she resisted, so I prodded her flanks, and then my hat went as a wind whooped down the draw, hitting us broadside so hard she crowhopped. I slid off, shaking, and gripped the reins, my lifeline in the dark. There was my hat, a dim glow in the darkness ahead. I reached for it and struck stone—a boulder, a mistake, the sort of place rattlesnakes hid.

I finally found the hat wedged in a stand of buck brush that scraped at me as I extracted it. I shoved it inside my shirt and snapped the shirt shut. I was able to remount by climbing the hillside and leaping across the saddle, but my hat got crushed. Lady took off at a gallop, as if she'd received her reward in a drink at the spring and was hellbent on getting home. We were halfway back before I got her stopped and headed in the right direction again.

She started up the valley with her head down into the wind, as if each step would be her last, and I could hear the fluttery clatter of the leaves on the oaks to my right. There was a break in the clouds, and for a moment I saw the treetops bending like whips in the wind. As we came over the crest of the hill, I had to gasp to get my breath; in my battle with Lady I hadn't noticed the wind had grown so fierce. It felt as if gusts of it would lift me from the saddle, and with a popping sound my bulging shirt flew open, and I grabbed my hat but spooked Lady, who seemed to be going sideways at about fifty.

I could hear the trees again and was frightened not so much by the shapes I imagined they were assuming as the actual whipsawing I had seen, and they were louder now. One could break off. Lady stopped. I slapped at both sides of her rump with the reins, but she refused to move. "Lady!" I yelled, the word tearing away, and she yawed to one side as if she would go over, then backed into the wind, her head down. There was the sensation of a hand smoothing the back of my shirt, and I swung around and slapped at it. Her blowing tail. No matter what I did I couldn't get her to move, and she started trembling underneath me.

"All right," I said, and slid out of the saddle. "You'll have to show me the way."

I stumbled through the dark, tugging at her reins, and occasionally she nudged at me as if to say she appreciated my getting down here with her. Wherever "here" was. I couldn't see the ground but could feel it, rough; my boots would be ruined if I got through this. She stopped, balking again. I turned my back to the wind, pulling at the reins, and ran into a barbed-wire fence. I put my hand out and felt a gatepost; in our struggle she had directed me here and was trying to tell me to stop. I got her through and cinched the gate up, and after we'd walked a ways I saw a line of light above us. It was a hilltop, and over its crest I saw gold shafts slanting from every window of the house and the barn at Siobhan's. Her father was scheduled to play the fiddle for her birthday celebration and dance.

I came across a boulder big enough to serve as a mounting step, leaped up on Lady, pulled out my hat, and held it on with one hand as I let her have her head. At the barn I leaped off in the midst of Lady's halting, as Siobhan's father did, but no one was there to witness this—a disappointment. I eased open a sliding door and saw Siobhan in the alley of the barn, in the calico shirt and tight jeans she often wore to church, standing on straw bales in a blaze of light.

"Well!" she said.

"Am I late?"

"Sheet! And don't bring that damn old clubfoot mare in here!" she cried. "Tie her up outside!"

I did, and Siobhan slid the door shut for me as I stepped inside, into warmth. I pulled off my mangled hat.

"That damn storm's about done it," she said, and glared at me with half-crazed eyes, as if I were the storm.

"What?"

"Daddy's in the house so drunk he'll be lucky if he sees Tuesday!"

What day is it, I almost asked, remembering her party was to be Friday night. I felt I'd been riding a month.

She strode over to the bales, the boots under her jeans swooshing in hollow, resounding columns as she seemed to kick her own ankles with the swing of her hips she'd begun to adopt. She leaped up on a series of planks laid over the bales to form a platform and then turned as if in expectation, her fists on her hips. I walked to where she stood with my hat in my hands, hoping she might teach me to dance or, better, allow the stormy correspondences I saw in her to break over me.

"That's it!" she said. "We might as well go on into the blame old house and tie this birthday off."

"*What?*" I was stunned to receive what seemed a sexual invitation, which, naive as I was, I was not so dumb not to pick up, and the jolt of it got me throbbing like a struck thumb.

"With Ma and the kids," she said. "End it!"

"Your birthday?"

"Don't you get it? Look around you, buddy! You're the only damn person here!"

So we wait out storms only to be reminded of their power to isolate, a knowledge that's been borne in on me further as I've spent this time to gather these pages out of a present upheaval. After that summer night, no storm in or out of nature ever threatened me as much, because Siobhan, in her dismissal of me, also had acknowledged my tenacity, or foolhardiness—the essential nature of one willing to strike through any upheaval, whatever its source, knowing there is always another side to it and knowing, too, what awaits one there: always another survivor.

🌿 Sleeping Over

She was sleeping over. This was in those days before the arrangement was commonplace, as the country moved from the edge of the melt of the cold war into Kennedy's sun, and there was nothing in her attitude, either at first or later, that would have led him to believe that she'd do it. There hadn't been a pact between them or even the suggestion of one, as seemed necessary then, or an exchange of promises, or a tendency to bind each other by any assent that he could trace, looking back on it, just the wallop of that mattress.

Then the sun-burnished breadth of her undone hair in the heat of the morning beside him. Something was settled between them and rose from them both as they turned to others, able to do this now, as plants that receive water turn and rise in the light that they must experience as their route to infinity. He felt, for the moment, freed.

They slept in the basement of the house, an aging place he had leased with a pair of friends and then discovered he couldn't keep up on his third of the rent. Friendship can bear most any hardship as long as it isn't attached to a dollar sign, he thought. Few friendships can bear that, and never when the people are young. This was a truth that unfolded in him in bitterness, from the area of abandonment (as he saw it) that his family had left. One of his friends was the overseer at a cyclotron and the other a draftsman and entrepreneur busy making deals, besides working on a doctorate. The two looked on him with contempt, he sensed, underneath their bafflement, and he, mostly trying to get his bearings, felt himself give with a guilt so complete he was embarrassed to hear the sound of his name.

He had come to the house with her one night expecting his friends to be in bed and walked in on a noisy party that had spilled into all of the rooms, including the bedroom that was "his." He wasn't made to feel welcome, nor was she, he saw, which angered him, since she was blameless, and after another drink, he went into his room, shoved the coats and mufflers piled on his bed onto the floor, wrestled the unwieldy mattress off of it, tried to center its crushing imbalance on his head, feeling his neck compress in a way he had to grind his jaw against, and swayed through the people he could see only in terms of shoes, or lack of any, turning and milling in the dining room; through the hall (where mattress corners caught and had to be pulled closer around him), through the kitchen, sending more feet into backsteps and turns, out to the back porch, panting, to the basement, where he heaved the thing free with a springy, unfurling wallop that sent dust billowing into the feeble glow that pulsed once when he pulled the light chain, then went out.

Light appeared at the windows from the house next door.

She had followed him down and stood behind him; she coughed, or pretended to cough, at the coal dust. It was enough, he thought, while he kicked at the mattress to get it out of the direct path through the basement, as if the party would soon extend here, and then got it aligned with the nearest wall; it was enough that she'd followed, to see him do this. She knew his friends and admired them; she was the daughter of a French Calvinist banker to whom unpaid debts stank of reprobation and understood their attitude and seemed to empathize with

him, too, as if she'd lived on the opposite side of the ledger
enough to identify with those who found themselves there,
because now she put a hand on his back as if to say, I'll take
this on for you, I'll help settle it. And at her unexpected touch
beside his spine, which the mattress had compressed so much
it seemed to be sprouting from his skull, he felt pressed into
forgiveness, healed.

He was lying facedown on the mattress. The party above
appeared to slow and dim, and there was a sudden rustling in
the darkness, and then she sat beside him and began to stroke
his hair, and from the spreading boundaries of her scent he
knew that the rustling hesitation had been to remove her coat,
if not more. He wanted to acknowledge this, to say something,
anything, but couldn't. He felt that dimmed by thwarted possi-
bilities and partial consciousness: guilt. He had fed on his inwardness so much that everything he took in, including sun on
a sidewalk, entered in darkened tones. He might manage to
make it through the remaining months and receive his degree,
if he wanted more debts, or he could take a job of the sort
that had been offered to him. He worked part-time as a studio
musician, improvising jazz, and could hire on full-time, but
considered himself a composer more than the machine that ran
the instrument. And he wasn't sure anymore if music was what
he wanted. He needed a rest, a caesura between the headlong
rush from early school and music lessons to his degree, which
was to tie off those seventeen years and act as a kind of insurance, too, in case his talent wasn't "rewarded" as his family
hoped. Or as they imagined it would be.

His family had said as much and suggested he get a job,
experience the world that way, and then they removed their
props when their circumstances changed; no more money. It
was the only time he'd needed them in an absolute and measur-
able sense, he wrote, and encountered such a blankness, he felt

not only abandoned but turned upon or cast out, an Esau.
Crybaby blues, he thought, and entered an explosiveness he'd
had to contain as the earth contained its core, though he was
able to let the explosiveness run through his head like a wail.
A precursor of the coming age, he thought. But before he'd
even got off on this strain, her hand was on his back, as if to
say, I'll take this on for you, I'll help settle it, as if the caesura
were possible through her, sending light down into his tunneling inwardness, and then she was at his head as if to accomplish
this.

Heavy head, she whispered, or so he heard.

He wasn't shrinking or helpless; he had a tongue whose
roots went into a darkness deeper than any he knew, and he
could be as resourceful as a cat to serve his own needs. He knew
it was up to him to stand guard over his complexity, or whatever
it might be called—that inwardness that had never fully formed
or tasted the outer atmosphere—which was like an oily mill
producing an essence at his center that seemed to govern the
pulse of his blood. He was the only one who could stand guard
over any alien influence, a killing theme, and keep it from
simply drying up.

But lately the turning of the mill had devolved from its
usual variations into a single note of *I, I, I*—attractive to some
in its insistence, but blinding to him. Fragments of experience
entered in chunks, in a precipitate that had to be beaten fine to
conform to the essence, or didn't enter at all, isolating him
further. And his self-consciousness, which he had taken to be
his way to eventual freedom, had turned into a kind of copula-
tion with a mirror, and about as gratifying.

Her hand on his back seemed to move through his body to
that source at his center, stirring up colors at its edges, and then
remain, as if in promise of more. He dropped onto the mattress.
She was at his head, his head in her lap, saying his head was

heavy as she stroked his hair, saying she loved his hair, which made it feel a part of him again, not a wispy adjunct, with roots fed by arteries that branched from the essence as it rose and pooled. Her hand penetrated and sent waves across it, like the ones that widen into sleep, and then she stretched out on the mattress beside him.

Then to wake in the light that came in dim shafts through a pair of sunken windows at the summit of the basement wall—a shaft on her hair, igniting it and seeming to burn fine its separated strands to a bloodlike core—and to see the laundry sink above him and beside that the wringer washing machine that had been here since the three had moved in but had never been used, while a wisp of a dream left his mind so white that it seemed he'd been rendered transparent, because he felt scrubbed down his length, agitated under suds and heat, rinsed and wrung out; pure.

She lay at his side, breathing heat over his face, her hair covering her features and tangled over her open mouth, her curled hands under her head, the short coat over her torso; and then her eyes opened, and she looked out at him from behind her veil of hair with an animal's questioning look from its place of hiding toward the potential of its master's authority.

He got up and went over and hooked the basement door, and the effect was as if he'd proposed.

They lived in the basement. It was spring, and sprigs and spears began to rise above the bottoms of the windows, tinting the morning light they lay beneath as they awoke in the subterranean atmosphere of the basement—this submarine bearing its fleshly cargo through each day, its windows dripping steam or rain. Her bicycle would be leaning against the washing machine, and the glint of its infinity of spokes in a shaft of light was like a representation of her fixed and radiating constancy—a reminder of the ordered source of the sun.

Two of his jackets hung from a rigged clothesline, and above the jackets the joists were woven with webs, which recalled to him the warning not to fashion garments from webs—was that it? He couldn't remember where he'd read this, if he had, or if it was an extravagance written in him by the conjunction of his jackets and the bars of the rough-cut joists, with their weavings to the natural world. The bulb, on its twisted wires to one side, was like the single thought worthy of contemplation: *her*.

He would fall asleep with that thought, and if she rose before he did and tried to slip off, the tick of her bicycle would wake him as she wheeled it to the door, sending sparking showers of light cartwheeling over the wall.

"*Tut, bicyclette,*" he would hear her whisper, as if her power to quiet extended even to the mechanical world.

Twice a week he put on one of the jackets and walked to the studio to work. He was a trumpeter, and now when he hit his highest notes he felt her enter like a messenger from Gabriel, expanding that dizzying blankness in him that came from bearing down on the last of his breath, as his fraying consciousness ascended the glacial scale to a flashout. He was approached by a wavering figure who looked paper-thin and asked him again if he wanted to work full-time. Blood beat in inroads at the edges of his sight and caused his tongue to thicken with numbness. "Gone," in musician's parlance. He realized he was being made an offer so generous, there wasn't a chance for evasion or his usual qualifications; he had to decide.

He held up his fingering hand as if to say, Let me get my breath first, at least, please, you see— And then he heard himself respond, from the rim of partial consciousness, "I won't be back."

"What's that?"

"I'm not coming back."

What he wanted, he knew now, was her. He bathed in the laundry sink, and she washed out his clothes in it, and the startling clash of color he sometimes glimpsed among his socks and trousers would be her undergarments. Both of them were always gritty with coal dust and drenched in the high acidic aroma only a blonde imparts, even on her breath, which her high carriage on her long legs seemed to epitomize, and she was sensitive to his seeing. She covered herself when she stood. He copied out a poem that begins

> *I wonder by my troth, what thou, and I*
> *Did, till we lov'd? were we not wean'd till then?*
> *But suck'd on countrey pleasures, childishly?*

He sat up after midnight until he had it memorized and in the morning handed it to her as though he'd stayed up to write it. She read it through and then turned on her back and shifted the paper in the light, as if to take in even the idiosyncrasies of his hand, her flesh shifting as she did, and at last said, "Donne. *Merci.*"

He took her to the premiere of a show in which he was to have played first trumpet (but had left at the time he quit his job), to display her to his musician friends; it was warm-up time, and they responded with an applauding clatter and honk that made him so uneasy he escorted her out before the end of the first act, when the houselights were low. He hadn't thought of her as a threat. He started working on something he called "The Wail of Old Gabriel," using only his mouthpiece, to spare the friends upstairs, but couldn't find a theme. She came across a nestling in a neighboring yard and brought it down to the mattress, trying to calm it as she held it squawking in one hand—an ugly, speckled, overbeaked oddity she said was a gackle.

Grackle? he asked.

It would never survive, she said, out of its nest.

He rummaged around in a pile of odds and ends in a corner of the basement and found a rusted cage ("This rusty, leaving cage of ribs" came to him, in the voice of one of the poets he'd been reading) that might have held a hamster once and which providence had placed here for her. They kept the bird in it. The thing stood on one foot, then the other, its head down and craned sidewise, blinking at them, a personality, and kept up a constant racket—to be fed, it seemed.

She carried it handfuls of grass and insects she would stalk and catch, then got an eyedropper and brought down a half-pint carton of milk every morning and fed it from that. They beat on the back lawn with the palms of their hands in an imitation of rain to bring up earthworms, and she fed the adhesive clumps of them to it. By now it was hers.

"*Ma petite*," she would say as she took it out, and then, with her head bent over it and her mouth shaping a kiss, she'd break into a torrent of affectionate terms that turned him away in embarrassment. It was the end of the two of them alone, and he was surprised not to feel diminished at this: a party to her concern for a bird.

Then she had to be gone for a day and left the responsibility of the fledgling to him. She helped him stock up on food, and he spent the entire time she was away in the basement. He fed the feather-clashing, airy thing with trembling hands, convinced that if anything happened to it, she would leave, since he knew by now that he needed her as surely as this bird pecking at his fingers—how could she take this?—needed food and drink.

He used the eyedropper, wasn't sure whether the bird had had enough, and then used it until he saw blue-white bubbles begin to blow from its gaping beak. He put it back in the cage and left it alone, afraid of what he'd done, and lay on the mattress until she returned with spring air over her hair in the evening; and when he awoke the next morning, he knew by the atmosphere in the basement that the bird was dead.

She was talking to it still, in an altered voice, and he heard her say it was her fault. His heart stirred and throat ached like its feathery stuffed craw—the greed of his overfeeding, the beastliness of it. He'd killed it, he knew that, and as quick as that he knew he could never tell her.

This was in that era when parents had all but complete control over their offspring, and her father had been alerted to something amiss by her diminishing bank account. He asked for her weekly schedule and told her she was to be in her room when she wasn't in class, and then he began to call at odd hours to make sure she was following orders; and her fear of her father seemed the force that would separate them for good. Family again, which brought up the bitterness about his own and revived the friends upstairs, as if from oblivion, with handfuls of bills and further demands.

She lent him her bicycle for transportation while he looked for other work, which he began to have to do in order to balance her account, and now when he awoke, the bicycle was like a reminder of promises broken, though none had been made, of course. She wasn't supposed to see him, but didn't keep this part of her orders to the letter, quite, and let him stop by on his rounds to talk, never herself, eyes averted, her back usually to a wall. One night, as she handed him a cup of coffee, he kissed her on the mouth. They rose, joined by the kiss, as if across a stretch of space of their days apart, and then he set his cooling cup of coffee down.

No, she said, and sat on a couch, her head bowed, submissive to the authority he'd never encountered.

He sat beside her, lifted back her hair, and kissed her again, feeling fallen strands entangling with their lips and tongues. And through his closed eyelids, as if seeing through flesh into her, he saw the basement around them in its stillness, the windows and the sink and the washing machine, the bulb above, and then the mattress, which she also seemed to see and be drawn to, because she began to arrange herself as if to lie beside him in the way her body turned and then stretched out to its length under the kiss.

They ran out into the cold night, no time to waste, in a line as straight as they could manage over lawns and down alleys and into a vacant lot where construction was under way and piles of bricks and girders rose up, giving off needles of light along their edges, and a wide excavation, with only footings poured in its depths—reinforcing rods splayed up like spears— suddenly gaped, and then they were there.

Then to wake in the tinted light to see her slacks on the line beside his jackets, dripping water near his head (the sound, he realizes, that has awakened him) from having just been washed; the array of the bicycle spokes across the washing machine, the cage in the corner, the bird gone; and to know that he would never hear for now those opening notes of Gabriel's theme, in this time of waiting, in those days when life and its opposite seemed fraught with absolute value, when his darkened consciousness began to be invaded by light, revealing first her and then the waking city around them with its variety of voices; in that year when lines of people backed for blocks around the Catholic church in the neighborhood, waiting to go to confession as the fleet of Russian ships plowed closer to Cuba; in this city where they'd met and he was sure he would lose her, finally, in the busyness of a crowd like this or in another; and then to hear, not quite in notes, from that revolving center in him: *She is sleeping over.*

✳ Confessionals

Some confessionals were of material other than oak, but they were so often of oak that oak is the wood that epitomizes them for me. When I cut into a scrap of oak with a backsaw in a miter box or run a length of it through the table saw, then work it with a planer or a rasp, I'm borne on its scent to those days when my existence seemed to center in a confessional. Confessionals were at the back of the church, where the aroma of incense seldom reached and a hint of holy water going stale in its stoup came from the vestibule along with a taint of woody mildew, as if from all the fingers dripping on floorboards over the decades, so that a bitter staleness beyond the usual still, stale air of a church presided; and there is no wood whose natural smell is so much like mustiness, if not urinousness, than oak's.

Carved oak spires or crosses often surmounted these confessionals, and most had lights or signals of some sort to let you know when they were occupied. It wouldn't be original of me to say they resembled coffins or caskets on end, with their heavy wooden doors carved to match the decorations above (or, in some cases, heavier doors of metal), and I say it because I never received quite such a feeling for what the otherworld of death must be as in a confessional. The door closed behind with a click. Inside, in a muffled hush of hanging velvet or velour, you were in the dark of the blind, with a padded kneeler, lower, for settling on to hold yourself in place. The sliding panel at your face shot back, giving you access to the priest, who sat between the two such "boxes," as they were also called, and you should have felt, ideally, that you'd been rendered an opening onto eternity.

The teaching of the church was that if you were in a state of mortal sin or had allowed sins of a severe nature to remain unconfessed, you could be consigned to hell—if you were suddenly taken, of course. The nuns who served as our instructors in the parochial school were artful at drilling this prospect into us. They were our real pastors and spiritual guides, since we spent six hours a day under their rule, and they taught us that the only way to be clear of these sins or to receive "the remission of eternal punishment," as our Baltimore Catechism put it, was via the confessional. An emphasis was punishment. "You'll suffer punishment for this," they would say, or, "I'm going to have to punish you for that." On the blackboard one would list the "most heinous" sins, in descending order, and describe the punishments, temporal and eternal, we could expect for falling into each. "For this, a boy was struck dumb. For that, you'll roast on red-hot coals in purgatory."

But if you looked up in the confessional through the window screen or latticework where the panel had been opened to admit a molecular glow, like nebulae at the edge of that eternity you faced, you could see the profile of the priest, and it was difficult to ignore the corporal (as the church referred to flesh) and imagine this person, whom you usually knew, conferring a punishment of such magnitude. He sat with a hand at his forehead, shading his eyes, or with a thumb at his cheek and his fingers at his hairline in a shield, and you were aware, only inches away, of his pomade or shaving lotion or his breath cloudy with wine if he'd just celebrated mass, or the cigaretty redolence that meant he would be in a hurry and wouldn't grill you like some—a good confessor to catch.

I was conscious, anyway, of his attentive listening as I whispered off my usual list for those years. "I missed my morning and bedtime prayers seven times. I disobeyed my parents five times. I fought with my friend twice . . ." The atmosphere was of complicity as much as penitence and then, as the formalities of absolution began, relief. This was over for another week, and I was about to be released, before those who were waiting in line outside or in pews at the back of the building began to imagine I must be involved in something awful to stay in the box so long. It was at the end of one of those sessions, when I had seen my confessor's hand sketch the sign of the cross, which meant absolution, and had watched, in the dim radiance, as he turned his confessional stole from its purple side to its white to picture this, that the priest, who knew everybody in our little Minnesota town, leaned close and whispered, "Tell your dot, Chonny, dat ve'll be playing pinochle at da parsonage tonight."

I got out of there as you get clear of a falling tree, and my own fall from the Catholic church, as it might be seen, began with my exit from that confessional. I'd never thought the mundane could enter that sanctum, and I was so upset I forgot to tell my father about the pinochle game; a parishioner came running over, later, to say it was on. There was only one telephone in our town in those days, the early fifties, and it was in the parsonage of the priest. He seemed the recipient of all incoming news.

One summer we visited relatives across the line in Wisconsin, south of Minneapolis–St. Paul, in the hilly, sandy landscape behind the rock bluffs that rise along the east bank of the Mississippi. Bushy junipers, jutting from the face of the bluffs near its top, look like buffalo in the act of leaping over, as my father pointed out when we drove by. He was a county agent—"the fellow who sits in an office and tells the farmers what to do," as he described his work. He said this area had been so poorly managed that the farmers were abandoning it; the forest had been cleared in the time of Ma and Pa Ingalls, who had lived here, he said, and the land hadn't supported farming since. There had been attempts to establish cultivation, once the trees were gone, and a few orchards had been planted, and then dairy cattle were turned loose to wander over the hills, and now the hills were washing in sandbanks over the roads. It was a disgrace, my father said, as he said every time he saw this; a disgrace. He'd reached the age when he seemed to repeat everything he said. Or I was at the age when this quirk of his was what I noticed.

A rural Congregational church across the road from our relatives' farm had been dissolved that spring, and as former members could find time over that summer, they were dismantling the building. We were greeted by my aunt and uncle, my father's sister and her husband, and their two sons—gawky, slow-moving boys—in the farmyard. Then all of us looked across the road with grim satisfaction, good Catholics, at another unwarranted church gone. Under shade trees, two men were prying off siding in the waning light, and another, notable for his width of white shirt, sat in a pew dragged under a tree, his arms crossed, staring back at us.

"Someday they'll learn," my aunt murmured in the exact tone my father used those words about farmers. She was referring, of course, to the departure of these people from the Catholic church, the one true faith, as if it had happened yesterday. "*Maybe* someday they'll learn," she said in amendment. There was the real rancor of visceral engagement in religious differences then.

Larry Woiwode

The next afternoon, when both sets of parents drove off for
the Twin Cities in our car, my cousins and I went across the
road to the church. Question 206 in our catechism stated, "A
Catholic sins against faith by taking part in non-Catholic worship because he thus professes belief in a religion he knows is
false." We had also been instructed by the nuns that it was a
sin merely to enter another church, and I never had.

"Hey!" my cousins said as I went up the steps, and it was
like a dare; I had to assert my difference. I entered the long,
stablelike building with more fear than I ever entered a confessional, feeling the prohibition cling to me like the air in the
building, as chilly as winter air, after being in the sun. It wasn't
a church anymore, clearly; the interior was gutted. Boards from
a wainscotting being ripped out lay in piles, in light that entered
in slanting beams from windows on one side; otherwise, it was
as bare as a roller rink. My first impulse was to tear it up more,
and then I heard my cousins come padding up behind me. They
were both barefoot; they always were. I noticed then, against
the far wall, above a platform, a row of tall wooden pipes.
"From that old organ," a cousin whispered, sensing where my
eyes were.

I'd never been in a church where I could make noise, so I
whooped and shouted, hearing my cries reverberate in deep
tones from the organ pipes. Then I tapped the nearest cousin,
initiating a game of tag, and as we ran and dodged from one
another in the bare building, boards screeched like birds, actual
birds flew out the open doors, and whenever we paused, I could
hear the pipes resounding above. I got up on the platform,
grabbed a piece of drape material from the floor, pulled it over
my shoulders, and turned to my cousins, who were younger
and had the gullible girlishness, as I saw it, of those who had
the misfortune of growing up on a farm. "Okay," I said, "I'm
the priest, and you two are altar boys."

They folded their hands, knelt in front of me, and we began a version of the mass. Halfway through one of my made-up speeches, in a language that approximated pig Latin, I sensed an arrival as if through the pebbly window whose shaft of light I was standing in—this was blasphemy. I was committing a mortal sin. The image that the nuns' pronunciation of "blasphemy" had always conjured up, of a blast furnace in the hottest iron regions of hell, now applied to me, and I understood why they had never explained the sin further when I'd asked. They didn't want to offer any opening in its direction.

I waited for the stroke of judgment, fully expecting it now that I was so far from a confessional, and my cousins, who'd been prostrate, pounding their fists to their chests, rose up and, like the animals they partly were, read this in my look. They turned to the doors, checking for witnesses, and took off as if the "It" we fear in tag had materialized and was hot in pursuit at their backs.

When I work outdoors, I'm not so much aware of the sky as I am of the details its radiance makes apparent—a sprig of grass stubbornly green in the midst of a brindled patch of snow; the cross-grain knot in the butt of a newly sawed two-by-four and the sawdust that's drifted from it, like downy spores over the gravel below; or the rust on the head of a nail holding my shingling scaffold. Though I believe my tendencies run toward spirituality, I'm an itinerant laborer, and I've done everything from farming to finish carpentry to stringing power lines, ranging across the open country that stretches from Kansas to the Canadian border (east of the Rockies) and on into the Laurentian Shield. What I first noticed when I came into this country was the purity of color in the landscape, some shades of which I hadn't seen except in nineteenth-century French painting and didn't believe existed in nature. They do, I can assure you, which has aroused a greater respect in me for artists in general.

I've counted several dozen shades of brown and lavender across this countryside in the fall. There's a stagey thump that the virgin sod has here over unshaded ground, so unlike cultivated land, and in the surrounding painter's colors, in light undimmed by pollution, you can suffer the sensation of being on a sound stage. For a second you see the entire panorama as being constructed to contain you in its scene. Your thoughts grow in volume, as though to fill the unpopulated silence, and return in an echo; you listen for the prompter's cue.

I've done seasonal work in the East, too, but the sensation only arrives here; some of these states aren't a hundred years old. East of the Mississippi, most of the land is one form or another of farm or lawn, from one state to the next, except where forests remain, and on the floors of those you find hardwood decay of a kind you'll never encounter here. Here there are rows of planted windbreaks and scattered second growth along rivers and creeks—no more—and I sometimes wonder if the mulch of centuries of these grasslands hasn't refined the palette into ranges so delicate that the colors can't be taken in without relearning an original way of seeing. Coming into a city or village from the land, you squint against the garishness of manufactured paints. Yet these are the hues we've grown used to, in varying degrees of intensity, and are the only colors most people see.

I said I'm more aware of details than the sky, but I have a greater consciousness of the sky here than elsewhere, with its particular angles of light across the working day, down through each season, and its expanse gripping every horizon. I've come to understand that the environment of the entire earth is sky. The sky here can assert an unbalancing effect if you stare too long into its presence of unpolluted blue. It seems to interpose itself between reality, like the silvery cast sunlight glosses everything with when you look out from a dark building, the world a mirage. I was sure, once, that my feet were set so firmly I couldn't fall as I looked up to study the sky, and then I was picking myself off the ground.

I was uninjured but forewarned, in a daze of the sort that I felt when I stepped from that church and saw my cousins running for the safety of their house. I had made it to the other side of a sin I never would have imagined I would be involved in, but before I was past the pew outside, which seemed to hold a stilled multitude, I began wondering how I could kneel in a confessional, whether I knew the priest or not, and own up to what I'd done, detail by detail, as I was expected to. Then, in one of those sweeping reversals that seemed my forte at the time, I felt that surely God—if He was all that I had been taught He was—would not hold a Catholic responsible for something he had done in a Congregational church, and one being abandoned by its own people on top of that.

I wasn't aware that my father was interviewing that day for a job as a foreman in a factory, but he was, and within weeks we moved. The town where we settled, south of the Twin Cities, was far from the hills where the farmhouse of our relatives now faced an empty lot, and the local Catholic church turned out to be a mission. It met at the outskirts of town in a wood-frame building that had once been a barbershop. During the first week of school, I began to court an acquaintance as a friend, and one rainy September afternoon we were in the basement of the public school during recess, playing marbles on its concrete floor, our circle drawn with chalk. He was lining up a shot—

an eye closed and his tongue curling from the corner of his mouth—when he relaxed enough to ask if I was coming to MYF.

"What's that?"

"You know. The youth club at church. We're having a party tonight."

"Which church?"

"Ours."

"The Catholic?"

"Catholic? Catholics don't have parties. They wear black and worship rosaries and dinguses like that. This is at our church, the big one, the Methodist."

He had taken his turn and missed, and now I thumbed a shot into the chalk circle, sending one of his cat's-eye agates flying while my shooter sat backspinning on the spot. You learned to play marbles in a hurry at our parochial school or your parents ended up buying a bag a week. "I don't think I can," I said. "I'm not supposed to go in to other churches." Now why did I say that? I wondered, and went back on my haunches, bedeviled at the thought of that other church, which, in the recent mixture of events, seemed the reason we had moved (so my father's pinochle partner wouldn't have to hear about it, in the logic my mind assumed), and found I was staring at a high gray window that streamed and ran with September rain.

"Not supposed to go in other churches?" a dim voice asked. "That sounds like some Catholic thing. You ain't Catholic, are you?"

"Yes," I said.

"Quit! Join our church."

"I don't think I can."

"Sure you can, if you want to."

"I don't think my parents would let me."

"You mean they're Catholic, too?"

"Of course."

"You mean you're going to stay Catholic?"

"I guess."

He grabbed up his marbles, including the one I'd won, and walked off.

Our mission was supplied by private-school instructors from St. Paul—a ragtag of priests and seminarians who drove out in a communal station wagon. The absence of Catholics changed me, and I still can't say after these years, with the sense of distance this country has supplied, whether the change was partly repentance or a strain of piety in me or perversity— anyway, I turned myself entirely over to being a Catholic. Devout, it was called. In the confessional, I gave the youngest and most lenient of our priests a sketchy account of that afternoon, and he slowly turned to me, as if to take in wholly what I was saying, and whispered, "Dear son, don't *worry!*"

I studied to become an altar boy and started to serve at mass. I was careful to assume the proper posture in my cassock when I transported the heavy missal on its wooden stand from the epistle to the gospel side of the altar, so there was no chance of tripping on its hem with that holy burden of The Book. I enunciated the Latin clearly and slowly enough so that I could meditate on its meaning within the mass. When I poured wine from a cruet into the chalice, I touched the last drop on its spout against the chalice's rim so it ran inside. I was diligent, during the offering of bread and wine, to grip the chasuble of the priest at the exact point at which the server on the other side gripped it, so that its silken or velvet material rolled in an even swag when the priest genuflected and then was like a sloping train as he stood and raised the huge host of consecration above his head. At the preparatory prayers of each elevation of the host and chalice, I rang the set of altar bells successively louder, to inform the assembly of the growing drama of the transubstantiation, and sustained the ringing at its highest decibels when Christ appeared as flesh before their eyes.

After months of this I realized I was spending more of the time I served in a dazed study of the carved and painted panel set into the altar's center. To the left was an oily gray ram caught in a bush, and on my side, or the one I usually served on, was Isaac, lying over a bundle of bushes like the one the ram's horns were entangled in, Isaac tied down with rope. Above, the hand of someone unseen reaches into the top of the carving to arrest the swordlike knife raised by Abraham, who is at the center of all of this. I had heard the story that was depicted, of course, but the carver who had set it in this panel had a sense of drama that kept drawing me back over its elements, as the priest's chasuble brushed one side or the other, for the meaning that would release me from my daze. I wasn't able to go quite so far as to imagine that the boy in the white robe, with one knee raised and a hand up in fear, was me, about to be struck through for those sins I felt were insufficiently confessed, but it occurred to me. Then Abraham's upraised hand was stayed. Who would do that for me?

Older boys sometimes served also—there were two large farm families that were our main supply of altar boys—and it was in the sacristy before and after mass, as we dressed in our cassocks and surplices (right on over your street clothes, in case you've wondered), that I heard my first off-color stories. Details from them would arrive while I served, assaulting me with specific intensity when I contemplated the boy on the bedlike altar with his knee raised, the knife in the air above, the terrible look on the face of the gray-bearded man whose arm was raised so far overhead that his robes were wrenched apart. And then that hand.

Before the priest was fully vested, we usually heard the scratch or rap at the sacristy door of somebody who wanted to go to confession. One or another of the priests came to hear confession on Saturday, but there were always those who couldn't make it or had been "on a Saturday night howler," as an altar boy put it. The priest would take out his confessional stole, kiss the crosses embroidered into it as he murmured Latin prayers, and then go out the side door, across the altar platform in four steps, and into the side door of a flanking room that was an exact duplicate of the sacristy. The confessional was here.

This is the last confessional I visited regularly, the last to rest at the center of my life, and in its improvised informality it was like an outpost in the direction the church was soon to take, with the advent of Vatican II. It represented more than any other the reality of our need to confess—a need some carry to psychiatrists and all of us to the person we love. A kneeler rested in front of a latticework screen constructed of strips of crisscrossed oak, and a linen cloth was draped over the priest's side of the latticework, to offer a pretense at anonymity, as bedsheets and darkness do. There was a wooden chair for the priest, and if you glanced down, you could see his shoes on the floor or hooked up on a rung of the chair. People in the queue outside the other door, which opened onto the main part of the building, would start up a foot shuffling and coughing if a priest or penitent spoke too loud; there was the sense of all of us being in this together.

The room was also a storeroom. Cardboard cartons were stacked haphazardly, as if to indicate everything deposited here or to remind you of the essentials needed for a journey to your interior. Storm windows or screens, depending on the season, leaned in a corner like the guises we put on to prevent intrusion while staring through them to speak those words we suspect others want to hear, and a mop stood in a bucket, for the wholehearted swabbing that would have to be undergone to really clear the decks—appropriate to the age I was entering. And all the cobwebs suggested those corners we don't wish to acknowledge or clean, or are blind to from familiarity, and were like the underlying apathy we string from project to project and confessional to projected confession.

Then the priest, behind the linen over the latticework—or at least the shadow of him as outlined against the uncurtained window at the rear of the room that opened onto the country-side at the edge of town. That movement above you, when you glanced up, would be a leaved-out branch nodding in the way the priest might nod or shaking a bare winter branch like a stick at you, and then a squirrel would come hurrying down the branch and look in as if to assure itself, yes, it was the same business that these human beings kept bending to. And on Saturday afternoons, or early Sunday morning, with the release of the weekend as palpable as the detergent-and-ammonia aroma present, the light from the north-facing window assumed a purity that seemed to hold the colors and shapes of nature in a transparent square that registered eternity.

So it wasn't much of a move for me to pass through that window into this countryside where I now work. I enjoy adding to the cables and pipework and boards and wires that more and more cover the earth in interlocking complexity. It is true that this open, inland country, with its scarcity of connections that form a gridwork over most of the rest of the United States, and with its stretches of miles between farm and ranch, and even greater stretches between towns and villages, has the feel, once again, of the frontier. Every connection here is doubly visible. It's understood that an examination of your faults and shortcomings has to be kept up, through the changes in every situation, if you're to make it from one day to the next among the people you're dependent upon. This implies trust, which is necessary in order to live and work with others.

The art of living, which is learning, presupposes imperfection, and we grow and develop to the degree that we're able to acknowledge the fine edge of the actual—instead of hardening in personal or popular opinions, which are mere opinions, after all. There are always those who will pick up their marbles and walk off rather than admit to any diversity, and we need to confess to them that prejudice, which always has as its standard some form of human perfection, no matter what shade the prejudice takes, is becoming too visible in this society that is turning increasingly international, or interstellar, to be passed on to the next generation with impunity.

As I hammer home a nail or wire up an electrical box, I'm aware that each act closes another link in the network that keeps closing the distance between us. I'm on the other side of the screen now, and no matter who you are, you're being drawn into intimacy with me; though by "you" I mean *you* in particular, the one for whom my smallest variation in inflection expresses a nuance of meaning unstated but understood. So that when I work under the open sky of one of these loosely populated places (only a million inhabitants in one huge state! six hundred thousand in another!), I sometimes feel your presence so tangibly I raise my eye from a detail—the tuft of grass with a pebble beside it as glassily pale as amber among the spores of sawdust—I raise my eyes not to the sky but to a meditative middle distance, and stand thinking these matters through once more, expecting your hand to come down on my shoulder.

Larry Woiwode

You were the one I intended to tell this to as though it were
the story of my fall from the Catholic church, and you are the
one who would see that it couldn't be so simple and that the
mixtures within the simplest motive provide the clues we need
to identify another's character—that personal trajectory we
each take through time. That trajectory at moments might seem
to be turning in a contrary direction, but it keeps to its course
over a path as predictable as a parabola. You understand this,
and you are the one who would have known, when I stated
near the end of this, "I felt I'd prayed among so many statues,
I couldn't pray anymore among people," that the statement
had risen from the defensiveness of youth, and that whatever
meaning it might have had then, other than youth's tendency
to deal in the generality of "people" rather than individuals, it
was now colored with a self-deprecating patina of twenty years.

And you do know all of this, and more, too, before I can
acknowledge that you do; and although I suspect sometimes
that it won't be long before I see you, I'm sure that when your
hand at last comes down on me, I'll probably swing around,
startled, as if the sky in its overarching span had united in a
flash my past and present, and I'll try to cough out these last
words: "I've been waiting a long time, but I never expected you
to get here so quickly."

80

❀ Blindness

"This can't be happening," Mel whispered, and felt his breath drift past his eyes in the cold. Once he and his daughter had walked beyond the range of the yard light, the landmarks he generally negotiated by had grown dimmer and dimmer until the ground itself darkened and he had to stop and stand, as he did now, with a hand out, unable to see. Or able to see only enough to guess that the layered shapes to his left were the branches of trees overhanging this part of the lane and the shifting area of light, lower and farther on, was his daughter trudging ahead in the self-absorbed strides of a four-year-old.

Then a crowd of silver particles, like a flock of startled birds, fluttered across his vision, and he wasn't sure he was seeing anything real.

"Evelyn."

"Yes, Dad." She turned to him, from the tone and angle of her voice—a responsive, easygoing child—and he thought he could distinguish, across the blankness between them, a lighter outline around the oval that must be her face. Her silver-blond hair, inherited from her mother. He shivered. It was early spring, cold enough for winter coats, although he had on only a jacket, and last night the crescent of the moon had rolled all the way under to new.

Was some faint illumination from behind, perhaps the yard

light, falling over her hair? He craned his head toward the house, resettling his feet for balance, and saw a smudge that seemed to rock as he watched, in the way the yard light rocked in a wind. But there was no wind. He turned back to his daughter. Black dark. He was afraid to tell her he couldn't see.

"Can you make out things all right, Evelyn?"

"Sure, Dad. What do you mean?" She might have moved a step or two closer, from her voice.

"You can see the road okay?"

"Sure, Dad. Why?"

"I wondered." He looked down and figured he might as well be on a coal carpet in a pitch-black room. He squinted his eyes but couldn't locate the tracks of the lane, which usually showed silver, no matter how dark. In his alarm he'd stepped out of the track he'd been walking in and wasn't sure whether he was off in the grass at one side of the lane or in the grass down its center. Leaf fringe, ferns, thistles—images of these sprang past, in a reflex to fill the emptiness, and he realized this had happened before.

In college he had worked two days and nights on a scale model of a theater, his senior project, and when he went out the second morning for a cup of coffee, early, the building he was walking beside seemed composed of particles that vibrated as he watched, and then every sense of color left his vision until the street and automobiles and trees were bleached gray. Then these began to waver, and it was only by force of will, it seemed—he was ready to cry, "Mom! Dad!"—that their colors started seeping back, and he leaned his hip against a car, trembling. Then everything was itself again.

Now he tested with his foot for one of the worn tracks. The lane led to a shallow river he usually drove their Jeep across, then drove back to the clearing where they lived. But lately he'd been leaving the Jeep on the other side of the river and walking, because if he started it up late at night (as he'd been doing for the past weeks, to go out for beer), it woke Evelyn, and she called to ask where he was going or started crying because he'd left her home. His wife had told him this, had suggested he park the Jeep where it was, and then tonight had asked him to take Evelyn along, as if to ensure his prompt return.

"Are you upset, Dad?"

"No," he said, but heard his voice go up and leave an opening—tentative and questioning—between them in the dark. He had been working on a set of plans for a city library over the last two weeks and trying to finish, at the same time, the plans for their own house; they were living in a house trailer until their real house was built. That house they had never got to, and he figured the set of plans would give them enough headroom to be able to bear the trailer for another year. He was doing commission work for an architectural firm in St. Paul. This week he had had to admit (though not to his wife yet) that if his proposal for the library wasn't accepted, he'd have to hire on full-time in the Twin Cities.

"No," he said again. "I guess your dad's getting old."

He meant to be lighthearted about this issue between him and his wife. He was older, in his early thirties, and lately, whenever he began filling out a personal check, he found himself thinking, November? January? April?—although he was usually fairly close to the date: the geometric clarity of numbers. He would glance up from the checkbook and find he couldn't focus. "November ninth," a store clerk would say, apparently familiar with his type. A certain personal music, as he experienced it, was seeping from him in a sort of internal bleeding; he no longer took the time to fashion the speeches he once had,

to put a personal edge on every turn of conversation—the badge
of ambitious youth. He'd begun to mumble, his wife com-
plained, and when they made love, he seemed to wrench a
muscle or pull something in his rib cage; or he'd lie beside her,
listening to her sleep, feeling an arm or leg trembling from the
strain.

"Old, Dad?"

"I guess."

"Did you say, 'Old,' Dad?"

Did she think he'd said, "Owed"? That, too, came up.

"I don't think you're old, Dad."

"That's kind of you."

"I think you look nice."

"Thank you, honey."

He had done more research for this library than for any
project, and it had left him feeling less spontaneous, and then
for the past three nights he'd been working over his drafting
board, with its adjustable fluorescents reflecting light into the
backs of his eyes, or turning to the drafting board behind, where
his expanding plans for their house lay taped—always keeping
a bottle of beer in reach and sipping at it enough to maintain a
displacing high. "An expensive job," his wife had said, "if you
count the beer. You see why I'm upset. You haven't been eating
well, either."

He felt chilled now, his tongue drawn against metallic dry-
ness, as if some cushioning element had been stripped from
him.

"Good Lord," he whispered, and his breath over his face
seemed to outline a sharpened form: a wedge. He no longer
knew what he looked like.

"What, Dad?"

"Oh, I was . . ." His work took its own direction, didn't it,
toward a tendency to abstract classical lines, as if the complexity

of a structure led him to its indisputable form? But lately as he worked a division of feeling entered him that obliterated his real self; he had traveled into a realm so far removed from his father, a laborer, there was no shield between him and his work. Or it seemed inconceivable that he received fees for doing what he had wanted since childhood, turning the shapes of daily life into further form, as his mother had done. Her structure of each day created the space their family occupied. The lines he put on paper, which became rooms where people lived, returned her structures to her and filled him with the pleasure he'd felt when he sat at her feet and drew on a tablet while she moved above him, always at work: her legs and shoulders, the arch of her hair, that perfect form he could never capture.

"What did you say, Dad?" Evelyn asked, and now she was so close she startled him.

Perhaps it wasn't her hair he'd seen earlier. He couldn't see it at all now. He felt her hands, sturdy and firm, grasp and tug at his right hand, and he let her take it in hers, feeling for a moment he was falling forward as he made blind passes with his other hand for her head. He found it and placed his hand over her crown, gripping the heat that rose from her hair, and imagined he could smell his wife's auburn outdoor health.

"Can't you see, Dad?" Evelyn asked, her head lifting under his palm to look up, and he was so relieved he had to laugh.

"Well, to tell you the truth, not really." Then, to lessen the possible effect of this on her, "I mean, with it as dark as it is, it doesn't seem I can see well."

"That's okay, Dad," she said, and gave his fingers a tug. "I'll hold your hand like this, and you can follow me."

"You think so?" He'd once said to his wife, "We're raising a mind reader. She knows exactly what I'm up to." And his wife looked levelly out of her sea-green eyes and said, "That's your fault." She intimated that he and Evelyn were too close.

"What kind of expression is it that you get when you sit there holding her like that?" she asked. He was unable to judge his own expression, of course, but her voice had called him back from so far, into such alien surroundings, he would look down at Evelyn in his lap, cradled in his arms, blinking sleepily up at him, and sense a stripped ache from his groin to the cords of his arches, as if she'd just poured out of his interior, as she once had, but full-blown, entirely formed in her present existence.

"Here," Evelyn said now, and gave his hand a shake. "Just walk real slow, like you do when you hold my hand."

He took some hesitating steps and felt his awkwardness and fear start up an internal amusement.

"You can't see, can you, Dad? You're not kidding!"

"No!" he said, trying to control himself. "Can you?"

"I can see almost like it's day out, but not as good."

"That's funny!" he said, trying to explain away his laughter. "You're funny!"

"Yes, Dad," she said.

With the directness of her answer he pictured his father turning to him from a floor where he was crouched, laying asphalt tile, and heard an astonished exclamation like ribald glee from him; his father had wrenched a knee, and this cry, a common response from him, along with grinning shame, was his method of admitting another physical limitation or an ache caused by age, as if he were saying, "I'm on my way out!"

Now Mel felt a sympathetic pain in his own knee and realized that his daughter was the only one he could give himself over to in entire trust. Then he glimpsed silver-toned trunks and limbs of trees, as if he were seeing through his blindness to a negative image of the countryside.

For whatever reasons the blindness had come, it was going, and for a second he got a glimpse of his daughter's hair.

He was being led from his blindness into a world that was the same as the one he inhabited (branches sprang into sight, unfurling leaves, saplings), but it was another world, and with his first tentative steps over its surface he understood the difference. This was the world of his daughter now.

❀ Silent Passengers

Shut it off, Steiner told himself, and the station wagon was silent. He had pulled into the drive and up to the Chinese elm at the house without the reality of any of it registering, and now he turned to his nine-year-old, James, in the seat beside him, and saw the boy's face take on the expression of sly imbalance that Steiner had first noticed this afternoon.

Steiner got out, and James bucked against his seat belt, holding up a hand, so Steiner eased back in, shoving his unruly hair off his forehead, and took hold of the wheel. He was so used to James being out of the car and headed across the yard the moment after they stopped that he felt dazed. His white-blond twin daughters, seven, who were in the rear with his wife, Jen, were whispering, and Steiner turned to them with a look that meant *Silence*. He got out again with a heaviness that made him feel that his age, forty-five, was the beginning of old age, and the remorse that he'd been undergoing now had a focus: it was that he and Jen hadn't had more children.

As he was driving home, a twin had pulled herself forward from the backseat and whispered that James had reached over and honked the horn while Steiner was in the department store, where he had gone to look for a shatterproof full-length mirror and an exercise mat of the kind the physical therapist had recommended. And since James hadn't spoken for two weeks,

the incident had set them to whispering about James, in specu-
lative and hopeful terms (with James sitting right there), for
most of the trip home.

"I'm sorry," Steiner said, seeing he was still the only one
outside the car, as if he had to apologize for being on his feet.
He slid back in, brushing aside his hair again, and began to
unbuckle James's seat belt. The boy stared out the windshield
with an intensity Steiner couldn't translate and, once free, tried
to scoot over to the passenger door by bending his torso forward
and back.

"Take it easy, honey," Steiner said, and then added for the
boy and the others, in the phrase he'd used since James was an
infant, "Here we are, home." Silence. Steiner turned to Jen,
who was leaning close, her pretty lips set, and said, "Do you
have his other belt?" She gave a nod.

Steiner got out and looked across the top of the station
wagon, through the leaves of the four-trunked elm, at their
aging farmhouse. He hadn't seen it in two weeks. He'd spent
that time at the hospital with James, first in intensive care, then
in a private room, where physical therapists came and went,
and at the sight of the white siding that he and James and Jen
had scraped and repainted at the beginning of summer, he had
to swallow down the loss he had started to feel when he realized
he was grieving for a son he might never see again.

He looked up at a second-story window and remembered
waking, sweaty, from a nap on the day that this began, on the
floor of the twins' upstairs room, where he'd gone to be alone,
and hearing James say, "Dad, do you still need me to help, or
can I go to Billy Allen's with Mom and the girls and go riding?"

"They're going now?" Steiner had asked, feeling dislocated
at finding himself on the floor of a room he usually visited only
at the twins' bedtime. He had climbed up there after downing
two beers in the August heat, and since he drank so seldom

lately, he had almost passed out. He and the family were back at their high-plains ranch for the summer, to get away from the silicon-chip firm on the Coast which Steiner partly owned, and he and James and a neighbor had been trying to start a tractor that Steiner wanted to use to cultivate trees—"to play farmer," as the neighbor said. Steiner and the neighbor had spent most of that hot August morning pulling the diesel tractor in ovals around the drive with a second tractor, getting it going for a while and then listening to it die, with James hooking and unhooking the drawbar chain and having to jump aside once in his nimble way when the neighbor missed the clutch and struck Steiner's big rear tires and merely bounced backward as the tractor stalled again.

Now Steiner strained to hear James's voice from that afternoon—the last time he'd heard him speak—and sensed that James had been at a distance, perhaps already heading downstairs, aware that Steiner was angry at the tractor and might be short-tempered after the beer. James would sometimes come up to Steiner, take his hand, and say, "Dad, I forgive you," before Steiner realized he'd been harsh or unfair, but James wasn't a do-gooder or tattletale: more a conscience.

Steiner had hoped to establish their home on this ranch and run his business from here, in order to spend more time with the children, as Jen had said he should. This last year he had been out of the office every month, traveling on consulting trips to Europe, and at the thought of all those jet-fuel-smelling 747s, Steiner was back on the floor of the twins' bedroom that August afternoon, reeking of the tractor fuel on his hands and clothes and the beer on his breath, caught off guard, laid low by drinking, and then he heard, as if James were standing above the spot where he lay: "I'll stay and help with the tractor if you want, Dad."

The memory of Steiner's response went through him so

wildly he felt as dislocated as after an electrical shock. What was it he'd said? "I don't care."

He realized Jen had spoken, and saw James rubbing the window on his side, impatient to get out. Steiner hurried over and opened the door, and James grabbed at the dash and the seat, trying to propel himself from the car. Steiner squatted at the boy's level and took his hands in his. "Be patient a minute, honey," he said. "Remember your belt?"

The boy's hair was as unruly as his, and the sandy-colored curl at its edges needed trimming. James's eyes were nearly covered by it, Steiner saw, and then they rested on him in a dull love. Steiner coughed and felt a hand on his shoulder. Jen was standing above him, smiling—wisps of hair lifting from her forehead in a wind Steiner hadn't noticed until now—and the sight of her somehow enabled him to understand that he could endure handling James in the condition he was in on home ground. The boy loved the ranch so much that his usual good health appeared to get even better once they were here; he seemed to grow an inch his first week back, each time. Steiner lifted James from the seat, turning him so his back rested on Steiner's stomach, careful of the boy's ribs, and the heated weight of James against him had the effect of blocking the blood to his brain. His mind went blank, and he couldn't think who he was.

James started pedaling his feet in a spinning run in place, and Jen laughed and shook her head. Then she glanced around the yard and off to a blue-shaded butte, as if to make the landscape hers again, and looked buoyant with the breath she took, then wiped at the corner of an eye. "You're so dear," she said to James, smiling down at him.

Steiner had spent the last week trying to decide if James's sense of humor was returning, as when a therapist had helped the boy down a ramp into the hospital pool for the first attempt at one of the forms of therapy a pediatrician had prescribed and James, a natural swimmer, had become so excited at the sensation of water that he tried to run and fell with a splash. When the therapist and Jen, who got her skirt soaked, pulled him from the pool, James mimicked a hangdog look, and then, for the first time since the accident, contrived a smile, wry and lopsided, that caused Steiner to laugh.

James produced the same smile when he was on his next instrument of therapy—a stainless-steel tricycle—every time the therapist relaxed her control over the handlebars and he rammed it into a wall, reminding Steiner of the time a colleague from the East, a designer whose chips were as intricate as a gridwork of Manhattan, with each cornice and window in place in every building, was scheduled to arrive at the ranch and Steiner was on the phone, trying to contend with a local plumber who had promised to check their failing sewage system but now was pretending he hadn't promised *when* he would, and Steiner tried to say, "But we must have a bathroom," and was only able to get out "But . . . But . . ." And when he hung up, James came hurrying past—nearly impossible now to recapture this dancing half run the boy performed with such agility—and said from the side of his mouth, "Is your butt broke, Dad?" Once Steiner had begun to grieve for the James he had known, the grief grew worse when he realized that in the last year or so it had been James, as much as anyone, who had been able to cheer him.

Now Jen slid an arm between Steiner's stomach and James, passing the padded canvas belt around the boy's waist. She drew it snug and then buckled him in. James's closed-head injury, as the doctors called it, was in the rear-left quadrant, so his right limbs weren't responding as they should, and the physical therapist had demonstrated to Steiner and Jen how to grip the belt from behind in order to support James in his walking, which kept improving with his visits to the pool.

"Do you want to—" Steiner began, but Jen already had the belt, and James went teetering off, with her in tow, past the front of the car, as if on a beeline toward the last moment he might remember—the tractor. Steiner's daughters went past with their hair streaming back, laughing at the speed of James's walk and Jen's attempts to keep up. James was enamored of farm equipment, and the connection he might make to the person he had been before, Steiner had thought through the hospital stay, was the tractor. Their neighbor had fixed it—a plugged fuel filter, he discovered—and had driven to the hospital to tell them when James was still in the state the doctors called comatose, and Steiner was sure he'd seen James respond.

So all through the hospital stay, Steiner kept telling James they would get the tractor going as soon as they returned home. He was grateful to Jen now, though, that she had taken him away. Steiner tried again to hear James's voice asking to go to Billy Allen's that afternoon, and then he remembered waking a second time, after the family was gone from the house, to somebody calling his name—the neighbor who had been helping with the tractor. "Billy Allen's on the line," the man had said, and Steiner's first thought was *Something's happened to James*. The neighbor was in the kitchen, staring out at the tractor, Steiner saw as he went by, noticing the broken-open six-pack on the table.

"Yes?" he said into the receiver.

"Steiner," Billy Allen said. "Bad news. The kids was back from riding, unsaddling the horses—your wife was there, I wasn't—when my gelding, Apache, spooked, I guess, and went over the top of James. He's hurt. I don't know how bad, Steiner, but he ain't conscious yet." Allen's voice parted with fear at this. "I called the ambulance. We'll meet you at the hospital," Billy said, and hung up.

Steiner called right back, but the phone kept ringing. Billy Allen lived on a river-bottom ranch thirty miles off and all summer he had been asking the twins to come and ride, and Steiner's response had been, "What's wrong with our horses?" until Jen said, "Surely you know that poor lonely old bachelor dotes on girls." So why did James go? Steiner almost yelled into the phone that kept on ringing.

He drove to the hospital at a speed his pickup probably wouldn't recover from, trying not to picture the ways James could be injured. He had bought the six-pack on an errand to town, for his neighbor to enjoy in the heat, he told himself, but back home he cracked a can himself, irritated at that damn tractor that had already cost him enough, and then looked down to see James staring up in sadness, prepared to forgive him. Then he recalled that he had told James on the trip to the ranch that he wasn't going to drink this summer, not even a beer—since lately drinking made Steiner unpredictable. The image of James staring up, with Jen's beauty in his features, stayed in Steiner's mind throughout the twenty-some miles to the hospital, while he kept saying, "Please, please," meaning, Don't let his face be disfigured.

He beat the ambulance in. The nurse at the emergency desk, wearing an orange stopwatch on a cord around her neck, seemed the bulky focus of a world that was still stable. She said the ambulance had called in, and from somewhere under the counter between them a radio crackled on, and an amplified voice said something Steiner couldn't catch. Before he was able to ask the nurse anything, she picked up a microphone from under the counter and said, "How is he?" A wash of static went through Steiner like anxiety, and again he couldn't make out a word.

The nurse studied him with set lips, appraising him, and said, "There are no marks on him, they say"—as if she knew what he needed to hear—"but he isn't conscious yet."

Now Steiner saw James swerve toward the granary near the drive, with Jen keeping up and with one daughter holding James's hand and the other grabbing at her mother's skirt. The tractor sat in the unmowed grass ahead. Steiner turned from them into a flash like a press camera's—the mirror in the rear of the station wagon reflecting sun into his eyes. He leaned against the automobile, unable to stop this sequence that kept returning: the stretcher tilting from the ambulance, James's blue face against sheets, Jen squalling up in the station wagon and running over in riding denims, the girls running after her, and then the glass doors to the hospital springing open with a hiss; hearing this and the clattering of the footsteps but no sound of a voice. Then the stretcher rolled close, and he could hear James going, "Ohhh, ohh," in shallow sighs. Jen embraced Steiner with an impact that set him off balance and cried, "It's my fault!"

"No," Steiner said, holding her so hard that the snaps of her jacket dug into his chest. The stretcher paused, as if the ambulance attendants were waiting for a command, and Steiner turned, one arm still around Jen, and tried to locate James's hand under the blanket and discovered that he was strapped to some sort of hard-plastic carrier. Two swelling, padded curves gripped his jaw on each side, and straps were buckled across his forehead and near his neck.

"It's Dad, I'm here," Steiner said, and thought he heard a catch in James's breathing. Good God, he thought, and closed his eyes and understood that each "Oh" from James was an attempt to cry out in pain and felt that if he could enter James and bear this moment for him, his son would rise from the stretcher and walk away. Then the doctor, a French Vietnamese who had taken over a local quarter-horse ranch, was in the midst of them, looking like a jockey in a torn red T-shirt, saying to an ambulance attendant, "You thought a spinal injury?"

He quickly undid the buckles near James's neck to help him breathe more freely, and the attendant said, "In case."

"Here," the doctor said, and grabbed the head of the stretcher and pulled it into a side room himself—as if to be free of the attendants—and over to an examining table. "Dad and Mom, here," he said, and when an attendant with a full beard attempted to block the door, he called, "No! I want them in here to help—answer questions! What's his name?"

"James."

"James! Can you hear me?"

James lay inert, expressionless, ivory, and beneath the overhead lights Steiner saw the boy's lips tug and quiver with inner pain, as if bearing it took his entire concentration. The nurse helped the doctor slide James and the board onto the examining table, and the doctor probed his neck and skull and took a flashlight from the nurse and looked into James's eyes, drawing his lids high with a thumb, and then, with a tool, scraped the soles of both feet, hammered at James's knees and elbows, drew the tool up his sternum, and said, "Get upper X rays, quick."

To Steiner he said, "I'm going to give him some oxygen through a nasal cannula here," already tearing open a sack. A coil of blue-tinted plastic fell from it over the boy's bare legs, pale and dirt-smeared. Why was he wearing shorts to ride? Steiner almost shouted, and felt a hand on his back. Billy Allen stood with a hat over his chest, chin trembling, and said, "I should have been there to help. Call my insurance company. Sue me." The elderly man looked almost in tears, and one of the ambulance attendants led him away into the hall.

"That's all I can do," the doctor said. "I see head injury but no sign of it. He's not posing or putting on displays of extensive damage, but is comatose, you see. I'm running quick X rays"— the machine above them clicked on, humming, and the doctor glanced at it and shrugged. "I'm sending him to the city hospital. You'll want all the attention he can—"

Steiner swooped for James, who had grabbed the side of the table to pull himself over, about to fall as Steiner got to him, and then, in a spasm that drew James's knees near his chest, he gagged up watery stuff, then groaned and gagged up a dark spoonful the nurse caught in a stainless-steel bowl.

"Last meal?" the doctor asked.

"Lunch," Jen whispered, hoarse, and Steiner saw her on the other side, ducking the X-ray machine a technician was running on an overhead track, holding James's hand.

"Goodness," the doctor said, "look at him empty his stomach—good response. We'll have to keep his lungs clear. I'm putting in a stomach tube. Catheter, too," he said to the nurse, already through a leg of James's shorts with glittering shears and clipping off his stained T-shirt.

"Test that," he said to the nurse, nodding at the bowl. "Could be bloody tinged. Maybe internal injuries," he whispered to Steiner. "I'm telling you straight. You see he doesn't respond in any normal way. Oh—a hoof got him." A curved ridge of torn skin lay under the stained T-shirt, and James's high arch of ribs was dented in. "Ribs," the doctor said to the technician. "Poor kid." Then to Steiner, "He'll be prepped for the ambulance."

"Let's call a helicopter," Steiner said, and everybody looked up, as if the shout he'd subdued had come out. He'd heard that helicopters were being used in this sparsely populated territory to ferry people to city hospitals, and the thought of this had arrived with a jolt: *critical accident victim.*

"The ambulance is as fast, I bet," the doctor said. "And about as smooth a ride. I don't want him jarred too much till we get a CAT scan. His spine's okay, I think. I'll get him ready and can just about guarantee he'll get to the hospital fine."

A silence came, and as Steiner waited for further reassurance, he looked across at Jen and saw her head bowed over James's hand, which she held to her lips. "James!" she cried, "I know you can hear me!"

The boy writhed: tubes were in his nostrils, and one was in his mouth—hurriedly taped to his sleep-struck face—and he seemed to be writhing in resistance to the catheter the nurse was trying to insert; his hand swung at her.

"Good!" the doctor said, and took the tube from the nurse and tried himself, sweat running beneath his glasses until he whispered, "This is so hard with little boys," nearly in tears. "It's just that we got to have access to his functions. Oh, little boy. His heart is steady, good." A black-and-gray negative clopped into a white-lit frame. "Oh," the doctor said, "four ribs, at least, in this first X ray, but no lung puncture that I see. I can say for sure they'll get him there without a change."

"I'll ride in the ambulance!" Jen declared.

There were looks all around, and the doctor said, "I'm sorry—I think they have regulations. Is the driver here?"

"Me." A young fellow at the door in a baseball cap.

"Follow right behind," the doctor told Steiner, tucking a blanket around James. To an elderly nurse who was looking in from the hall, he said, "Ride along and keep him warm. And you," he said to the ambulance driver, "take it slow, easy over bumps, no use exceeding, play it safe."

It was the longest trip Steiner had endured, it felt, following at the ambulance's back, separated from James. But during it he heard the story from Jen. Billy Allen had been busy moving irrigation pipes, so he got the horses saddled and went back to work, and when they were done and had started to unsaddle, the horse that James was riding, Apache, went wild, Jen said— all of this happening so fast she hardly had a chance to get the girls out of the way as Apache charged. She was sure James was safe, because he had been standing farther back, and then the horse spun, its saddle swinging to one side, and she heard a sound like a post struck and came around the corner where she'd taken cover and saw James, a ways from Apache, hit down.

"I knew right away he was terribly hurt. The horse went off to a fence, kicking at the saddle, and the worst part of it, I mean now, is that James was on his back trying to push himself up. He's that strong. His head came up, he tried to open his eyes, and then he sank back, and I caught his head. I didn't think he'd breathe, I waited so long, I don't know how long, rubbing him and asking him to breathe—I knew I had to support his head—and finally he gasped."

Steiner saw that James had traveled past the tractor with his mother and was heading toward the pasture at the northern corner of the yard. The twins were going ahead, through shaggy grass that hadn't been mowed in weeks and reached to their hips, toward a garage that stood alone at that corner of the two-acre farmyard, the peak of its roof like a parody of the tepee buttes that rose above it—so hazy in the late-summer heat that they seemed to simmer on the horizon like a mirage. Then Steiner saw where James was headed. At the end of the garage, on the other side of the pasture fence that from his distance was invisible, three of their quarter horses—a stately bay the size of a cavalry mount and a buckskin mare who seemed on a constant nervous search for the colt nudging up behind her—came ambling forward, all of them at attention, their heads and ears up.

Then the bay whinnied in acknowledgment of the family he knew.

James was heading toward him.

He remembers, Steiner thought, his hair going back in the wind, and sat down in the seat where James had been sitting. Steiner had imagined taking a 30.30 to Allen's and dropping the rogue Apache. I still might, he thought, once James is—

The second night at the hospital, while he stood watch in the intensive-care ward as Jen slept, he heard the beeps of James's heart monitor start to slow, and when he checked the digital display that printed out every half minute, he saw it read forty-six. At forty an alarm went off, and the nurse on duty, who was at a desk behind glass, looked up. It was a large ward, but James's bed was the only one in it, and the nurse glanced at the monitor on her desk and then shook her head as if to clear it. She was Steiner's age, responsible for supervising the student nurses, besides her ICU duties, and Steiner understood by her response that she was overworked.

She came through the door into the ward, which was dimly lit by baseboard lights, and stood at the other side of James's bed. "Is our boy tired?" she whispered, and with the second sense Steiner was developing, he realized that her concern for James exceeded medical limits; she had become personally involved. She was wearing slacks and a turtleneck—the informality on pediatrics disturbed Steiner; nobody wore white—and he could picture her standing like this with her husband, the baseboard lights projecting their shadows on the ceiling above a son's bed. "Should his heartbeat be so slow?" he whispered, imagining James heard every word.

"Oh, he's a child," she said, recovering from whatever state she had slipped into. "It's surprising how low it can go in one. Did he use to run a lot?"

"Yes."

"If it was you or me, I'd be concerned."

But when she went back to her desk, he saw her turn aside to make a phone call. The next digital printout read thirty-five. At thirty Steiner saw her go to a refrigerator and prepare a syringe, and then he had to blink against the overhead lights she suddenly switched on. She walked in and looked down at James, her hands on her hips, detached and angry, a nurse again, then strode back to her station.

Steiner put a hand on the far side of James and leaned over him. "James," he said, and couldn't say any more. Without a sign of injury, James looked more beautiful than ever, and all Steiner could do was stare down at him and take in every feature and inch of skin in case he never saw him alive again. He felt he could see into James to the place where he had retreated, where his real self rested, hidden, and should call to him there. Then this seemed presumptuous, grandiose—as if it were in his power to call James back! His lips felt sealed. But if he, the boy's father, wouldn't make the effort, who would? "James," he said firmly, more severely than he'd intended, and with a skip the boy's heart rate on the monitor picked up again.

The neurologist was noncommittal, one neurosurgeon was hopeful, many of the physical therapists were encouraged, but the pediatrician overseeing James was pessimistic, given to scowling, and when James didn't fully awaken from the coma after forty-eight hours, and seventy-two, and then four days, his scowl deepened. Wriggling a toothbrush mustache as he pursed and compressed his lips, he asked Steiner and Jen "to step with" him from James's bed, where they were sharing a shift. He sat them down in a lounge and said that since they hadn't seen any of the signs in James they were looking for, all of them had to face the worst: that James might not recover, or if he did, he would have to undergo the most comprehensive therapy merely to restore his basic functions, which did not mean—his mustache wriggled—vocal speech.

They tried to convince him that they had seen a change, that James's eyes were open more often, that he seemed to respond to his name, that the head nurse had said she was sure he was following along when she read from a children's book she held in front of him, and Jen brought up a theory she'd mentioned to Steiner—that James was such a perfectionist, he wouldn't speak until he could speak as he used to. No, the doctor insisted, they must not get their hopes up; that was why they were having this "counseling session."

So Steiner got up and took Jen's hand and walked off with her to a room the head nurse was letting them use for naps, and in a rawness of intimacy he wanted to have her on the spot, but knew they must do something as parents. Without a word to one another, they went down on their knees. Steiner wasn't sure what he said but felt they were on an ascending elevator and when they stood had reached another plane. Then Jen said, "I want to hold him."

They went into the hall hand in hand and hurried to the boy's bed, like youngsters escaping the pediatrician. Steiner helped Jen draw James from the bed, moving tubes and an IV stand, and into a rocker with her. James's head dropped back, his lips apart and his eyes open, and he stared up at her with the distant look Steiner had seen in him when he rested in the crook of her arm like this as a nursing infant. Then James struggled to rise and put his arms around Jen's neck.

The next morning, as the pediatrician was doing his daily tests and called, "James, squeeze my finger!" he glanced at Steiner and Jen, eyes wide, and said, "Some grip!" Later that day, James opened his mouth to speak and looked puzzled, then tried again, shifting his lips, and finally gave up. But from then his progress was fast. The next day, he was transferred from intensive care and put on his course of physical therapy, and then Jen said it was time to go home. The pediatrician, who by now was less pessimistic, went so far as to say that Jen was doing more for James than most of the—there was a twist to his mustache—"care professionals."

So they left, and now, away from that institution and under this expanse of sky, Steiner understood that though he may have thought the worst at times, and didn't always know how to handle what was happening, there was a part of him that never doubted that James would recover. Which was what allowed him to stay sane enough to help the boy. James's recovery seemed an internal process, nearly separate from him and Jen, and they had been borne along by it, silent passengers, aware only of the movement of time overhead, until it had brought them home.

So now Steiner drew himself from the seat and walked around the station wagon to watch James and Jen and his daughters at the fence. The horses were arching their necks down to them, and James leaned forward from the belt, his left hand up, and stroked the nose of the bay, then the skittish buckskin, who jerked back at his touch, checked for her colt, then came forward and nodded her head at him. His hand traveled over her face and muzzle, unsteadily at first, and then he assumed a courtly stance that he used to favor, and Steiner had a glimpse of the son who had always had a way with pardon. That's enough, he thought. He had always wondered how parents with injured or diminished children were able to bear it. He pitied their patience and calm, but now he understood; it was enough to have the child with them, alive.

James turned, sensing Steiner's eyes on him, and brought Jen swinging around as she held to his belt, and the horses wheeled away, heading down the hill toward the pasture. *Get back,* Steiner cried to himself. He could feel the battering of hooves from where he stood and imagined the weighty charge of Apache toward James, and then a gust of wind took his hair straight up, and he saw James's and Jen's and the twins' hair climb the air also, the girls' high above their heads, streaming back like banners against the sky. And over the days and months afterward, when James had started talking and traveling everywhere on a run, the sensation of that moment kept returning to Steiner—all of them suspended for a second against the horizon, silent in the wind.

✣ Black Winter

Baldachin, Kiner heard, from a dormer of memory gold with riches, he sensed, but the word slipped down a dark hole. He stood at the kitchen window with his first cup of morning coffee, and his reflection in the glass, as pale as the blowing snow he'd been watching, seemed the source of the memory, and then his mouth, pursed in his silver winter beard, parted as if to— What? Beyond his reflection, he couldn't see any flakes falling, but a low layer of snow kept traveling across the yard, just above the grass he'd neglected to mow in the fall, its sheetlike layer of flight like a blizzard seen from above.

His inability to place "baldachin" made him feel so enfeebled he figured he might as well turn to philosophy, as old gents do, if philosophy weren't what he had turned from to begin with. If his memory was working, there had been only a dust of snow on the ground when he drove home last night, and until the mid-part of this month it had been a black winter, as locals put it. Some said "open winter," meaning the harvested fields were open to the weather (or that the roads were open, for those who had children in school), but the old-timers had the better term: *black winter*.

Snow was skimming across his yard now, though, forming a rippling surface like the surface of a stream a foot above ground, as insubstantial as molecules, although thicker streamers went flailing through the coursing current of it like veins of white water in a river going over its banks, and he could hear the upper story of the house creak and groan and the volume of air in the kitchen shift with the wallops of northwest wind. It was only minus ten, but he had heard on the radio that with the wind chill it was fifty below. Now, all over America, newspapers and television announcers would be mentioning "cold arctic air moving down from Canada," as if Canada manufactured it. Americans seemed to believe that weather like this was Canada's daily fare, if you could take as a clue the way cabbies in the States shivered when Kiner said where he was from. Which he did only when these over-the-shoulder inquisitors—most of whom seemed derelicts who'd commandeered a parked car—pestered him: Winnipeg. Canada, he had to add, in recent years. I'm from there and I'm not, he might also admit, in his fussy philosopher's need (a remnant of his training) to be exact. I grew up near Winnipeg, but I've spent most of my life on the East Coast of the States. Teaching, he sometimes added.

But now he was back. He had "elected" to retire early, at the urging of a committee, whose wisdom, as they put it, was meant to free him for his own work. His production for the past decade, as the committee well knew, was a series of essays in journals so recondite that many no longer existed. What the committee wanted, he figured, was access to his salary as an open line, so they could hire a junior professor at half his wage, and divvy up the remainder in raises to one another. Which is what they did, once he left.

He had thought he would teach half time, so that his free semester, hooked to the summer break, would give him eight months off; that was sufficient. But their "wisdom" was a request, he knew, and now he had so much time on hand that, after a year of it, his sense of the hours going past unformed, endless, was appalling, worse than Wittgenstein's silence. At sixteen he had gone to the U. of Manitoba, and from there to McGill, then to Harvard, for his Ph.D., and afterward put in thirty-six years in the American system, insulated by the self-absorption that his driven nature produced (which he, like every monomaniac, passed off as absentmindedness), so that he hadn't noticed how he'd come to depend on the order of that regimen to organize his life. He had, in fact, over his year at this place, finished a first chapter on that topic: the academy as the locus of formal structure to thought.

He went to sip his coffee and discovered the cup was empty. He wiggled it as if he could cause the coffee to reappear, and saw that the window in front of his face was steamed up, as if he'd been panting. Philosophy's waning hold had slipped from him in Europe, when he was forty, and had finished most of the work he was known for. This fall he turned fifty-eight, and it was a month since he'd sat at his desk. Mostly correspondence nowadays, anyway, over further cups of coffee. Or that was so until he'd taken this job.

By the numerals on his university-office coffee maker, he saw he was late again, due to this morning dreaming that was consuming more of his time, and in his rush to leave he almost dropped the cup, part of a set of his grandmother's china, into the dustbin. He got it to the sink, a shallow, tublike affair installed at a slant and stained with orange streaks, and rinsed it under water so icy that the portions of his fingers retaining sensation felt scorched. His circulation was pathetic in winter, as sluggish as the house's antiquated water system—which still served, though, in this rural isolation he had come to appreciate. He and his father had installed the plumbing in the fifties.

"Steven," he heard his father say, and turned as if his father, who had been dead for fifteen years, had walked into the room. "Steven, how many times do I have to tell you, don't hand me

one pipe wrench when a guy's got to have two of dem to work
dese pipes right!''

There was no sun that he could see in the suffusion of brilliance
he had to squint against. He lowered his head against the wind,
the hairs in his nose already frozen thick as sagebrush, and
shoved his hands, in the fur-lined gloves his chiropractor recommended, under opposite arms. Houdini bound. The undulating layer of snow flowed southeast below his knees, his
mukluks hidden beneath its powdery weaving, his feet trodding
on invisible corrugations, as firm as reinforcing rods, of beginning drifts.

The streaming snow drew him off course, and he thought
of his patrimony, as it might be seen—this farm that became
his when his grandmother, in her nineties, lost her life in a
storm like this, now a dozen years ago, on her way to feed her
hens. Kiner always suspected he would return, once he retired,
and when he arrived last fall, the only building he found fit to
use as a garage was the smithy his grandfather once worked in,
at the far edge of the yard. The distance to it, after leaving the
walk, was a hundred and ten paces, as he'd clocked it, in case
there was a storm in which he, too, got lost. He had hired a
carpenter to install an overhead door in the garage, and had
hoped to add a remote opener, later, but had discovered that
his cooling car, in the worst weather, melted the snow along
the bottom of the door so that it froze down. He had had to
carry a teakettle of steaming water out a few times to loosen
it. He'd known enough not to install an overhead door with
windows; when you tugged or pried at a door of that width,
your force went on a bias, and in the subzero cold the glass in
it went flying in the sparkling fragments of a detonation.

If you don't base a business on a religion, then the business itself can become your religion. It was Kiner's voice. He had said this on one of his first meetings with the young fellow, a Hutterite or Mennonite—a member of one of the local religious sects— who had asked Kiner to be his manager. "Just for a while," the fellow added. "Until we see how it's going. Six months, say, then we'll see."

The icy casters screeched up the overhead rails as Kiner raised the door on blackness. The door faced south, so the wind was wrong to enter the building today, but in the dark and quiet smithy it felt colder than the outdoors. Kiner clenched and unclenched his fingers—already smarting from the first touch of frostbite. The latch of the car door snapped with a delayed action that meant it was frozen, and the plastic uphol- stery was so cold he cried, "Oh!" In his hurried entry, he had shoved the towel he kept on his seat over the center hump. The engine caught the first time, a reliable Canadian product. He gunned it and then, with his door ajar, backed hurriedly out, in jerks, before the car was properly warmed up. The thought of carbon monoxide, alone as he was, scared him.

With the shift in park, he kept revving it, and then saw by the clock on the dash that it was nine—already an hour late!— and shouldered open the door in a rush that almost sent him sprawling as the wind flung it wide. Shuffling his feet for fear of ice below the gray-white stream, he drew the noisy overhead door down with a bang and, before he dropped onto the seat again, rearranged the towel over its icy plastic. He was out of breath. He drove down the drive and, near its end, where it sloped to the gravel road below, felt he was seeing a blizzard again from above. Then he remembered that he had thought of something at the window—perhaps a file or the insurance pol- icy he should take to town—but couldn't move past the act of remembering. His mind, over the last year, had come to seem a slippery well where beginning ideas dropped without a splash, while unbidden ones kept circling its outer walls like lizards or geckos on a nighttime spree.

On the gravel road, the ground-hugging current of snow, spraying up at the far ditch bank, hit at the bumper, and as he turned north, a draft entered the seal of his door and chilled him through his coat. The snow spread in a flat and undulating haze just high enough to obscure the washboards and potholes he usually avoided, but the road was straight, at least, and lined on each side by barbed-wire fences—like running a gauntlet. He was almost to the house of the elderly couple, as he thought of them—they had watched over his grandmother during her last years—and here had to swing west onto the road to town. But the coruscating layer of snow, running crosscurrent to the road he couldn't see, was so dizzying he wasn't sure where to turn. He switched on the heater, since it wasn't until here that it blew anything but an icy blast, and began to turn, cursing himself for doing two things at once, which was the surest way to get into trouble in bad weather. Then thought, No, I've done four: had the detachment to note I was doing two, plus the curse. He was still on the road, but had slowed almost to a stop.

Then he saw somebody walking the right shoulder ahead in stiff strides, his back to the car and his calves divided at their centers by the driven snow. Kiner pulled even and saw it was his accomplice, as he thought of him, Sweeny, the sixtyish fellow who lived to the east and was the sole employee of the business Kiner was managing—a welding and repair shop.

Kiner reached across the car and unlatched the door, and Sweeny wrestled it wide as if in a fury, admitting a blast of air that stopped Kiner's breath, and then little Sweeny flopped in on the seat and slammed the door. "My God, man," Kiner said. "This cold! You could kill yourself!"

Sweeny pointed a finger at his temple and went "Pow!" His teeth were twisted and lapped over one another at the front, a defect that gave his eyes, as he smiled now, a cross-eyed look. "The bitch killed," he said, and wound his mittens through his arms and drew his arms, crossed, over his chest. He was wearing only the work overalls and denim jacket he usually wore (though God knew how many layers of underwear he had on underneath), and his jacket emanated cold and creaked with ice as he hugged himself. The only clue he was cold was his nose, red and running over his lips.

"You could have frozen out there."

"I by Jesus came an inch from it, but I knew damn well you'd be your usual hour late."

"You should have called."

"Slog back to the mothering house to call? When I was down the lane! *Pfft!*" This was his trumpet of scorn, and with it a string of mucus went cartwheeling through the air and hit the dash. "The damn insurance adjuster's coming!"

"Right." Kiner felt rebuked. Though Sweeny could be recalcitrant, or worse, Kiner had come to depend on him for his knowledge of the business—if you could steer him past his prejudices, inherited from the former owner, a windy geezer named Trotmeyer, who never would have sold out, he told Kiner, "If the welding hadn't turned my eyes to mush."

Kiner drove on, willing to let Sweeny simmer, and then remembered to turn the heat on high. Now he was running at an angle to the flight of snow that the car seemed to float upon, and on this higher road its surface parted to reveal fins of white forming behind the biggest chunks of gravel. "What kind of weather is this!" Kiner exclaimed.

"A ground blizzard, dope."

"I mean, where is the snow coming from?"

"Yellowknife. *Pfft!*" The scorn suggested Kiner should know, and it surely wasn't Yellowknife. Though the low-traveling wind was obviously carrying it from somewhere.

"Do you think—"

"Leave me sleep!" Sweeny threw himself against his window, which was already frosting up, and closed his eyes.

Kiner wanted to ask if he thought Trotmeyer would vouch for their safety procedures to the adjuster. Trotmeyer was unpredictable, a Manitoban Lear, shaggily white-haired, six-six, with a noble carriage and hands that gestured in the downward sweeps of tragedy. He liked to lean close when he talked, right up over you, depending on your height, occasionally taking your clothes with a thumb, in a buttonholing more than an intimidating habit. Like any machinist who works steel to fractions of a millimeter, he loved to talk. On and on. The topic wasn't important, though Trotmeyer's favorite was politics, and his politics, to the taste of his customers—farmers dependent on the dole of supports—had a conservative stripe to the right of what was palatable. Trotmeyer had alienated so many of them, Kiner was sure this was the reason Trotmeyer had sold out, rather than his eyesight. Trotmeyer would go on a tear and start to orate, striding across his shop without a trace of the ungainly hesitance of those with truly bad vision, and little Sweeny would scurry in his wake, encouraging the tirade by socking a fist into his palm or crying, "Right!," or, "Let 'em have it!," soon to add, "Nuncle," it seemed, until the melancholy duo of them—

Kiner glanced from the snow-swept road to Sweeny and caught the fellow with one eye open, staring at him. It closed. Had Kiner been speaking his thoughts out loud? He had taken to that, though the car's atmosphere and Sweeny's response suggested not. It was ten miles to the shop, on the outskirts of a small town south of Winnipeg, and Kiner guided the car at a stately thirty-five through the snow whose sidewise travel more and more gave him the illusion of being afloat, the earth absent, whited out. Then Sweeny began a steady *Pffuu!*, *Pffuu!*, his lips

bulging monkeylike with each exhalation, a gentle snore—
felled by the heat of the car after the cold.

"Okay, I shouldn't have gone to the auction." Kiner had said
this to his lawyer, in the local coffee shop where they'd met for
lunch. "I saw the poster but decided not to, and then Sweeny
called." When Kiner was young, his grandfather had taken
Sweeny on as an apprentice, and Kiner had felt the heat of
jealousy. He often sensed that child coursing in him, bubbling
up through the strokes of his heart in a giddy— He looked at
Sweeny, ashamed by the age of them both. He used to love the
danger and fascination of the forge where his grandfather stood
and shaped a piece of rose-red steel, his shirt off, his chest and
stomach muscles dotted with scars from burns, dripping sweat
even in winter. Kiner had endowed him with the nobility book-
worms confer on sweating laborers, as the Oxonian Hopkins
did for the blacksmith who "fettled for the great gray drayhorse
its bright and battering sandal."

"There's no doubt Trotmeyer reminds me of my granddad
in some way—by occupation, not personality," he'd said to
his lawyer. "At the auction he kept declaiming how much
everything was worth." There were a hundred people present,
and when there was a lag in the bidding, Trotmeyer would
stand and hector the crowd. It was a fine place: four acres,
a capacious shop with double steel walls, insulated between,
packed with equipment and tools and materials and parts
enough to keep the business going for a year: a lathe with a
twelve-foot bed, a milling machine, drill presses and grinders,
two heavy-duty welders and two wire-feed, one on a pivoting
overhead boom; a field repair truck with a gas-powered genera-
tor and welder and acetylene setup and an array of tools in its
steel side boxes built by Trotmeyer; a plasma cutting torch, an

overhead crane, a forklift, a tractor with a front-end loader, an older pickup, an office with desks and files and a toilet separate from the toilet for employees, a trio of steel welding tables set into concrete, their grounds buried out of the way under the floor, two wide racks of raw steel, a hydraulic press that loomed over the auctioneer, with a huge open frame fashioned like a child's drawing for the game of hangman, but of twenty-four-inch I beams, with an open bed below that bent iron bars like butter—powered by aircraft hydraulics: another of Trotmeyer's creations. And with all this parked and lined up and laid out in the building, along with the crowd, there was room for a dozen more pickups.

"I didn't put money down blind," he said to his lawyer. "Sweeny told me if I got the bid, for up to fifty-five thousand, he'd pay me back the ten percent I put down when he got his loan, plus interest. Just the equipment is worth over a hundred thousand!"

"Did you get anything from Sweeny in writing?"

"Well, no. We're neighbors, sort of."

Kiner's lawyer attempted not to respond but had to look down at the ribbed glass sugar container he was turning on the table, as if to keep from rolling his eyes. "How many days until you have to come up with the balance?"

"Thirty days from the sale, November first, so—"

"That's a week!"

"About, I guess. Sweeny needed time to get around to the banks and try to work out a loan."

"Kiner, he's about— He's not near as reputable as Trot-meyer, and no bank is giving Trotmeyer a loan."

"What do you mean?"

"Maybe it's his eyes, but he's at a dead end. It looks like the business is. Sweeny's a worker, not a manager."

"What a situation!"

"So you bid fifty-two, minus the five-two you put down. Can you come up with forty-six eight?"

"What would I do with a machinery-repair shop? I've got my hands full with the house I'm trying to fix. Then there's my own work. I can't be in town full-time."

"Find an employee you can trust. Have me do the books. You said you figure anybody ought to be able to make a go of it, and frankly, with good management, I do, too."

"I could break into my annuity, I suppose, but that would cut by a quarter what I have to live on."

"Who was the next-highest bidder?"

It was a group, actually, Mennonite or Hutterite—Kiner couldn't tell anymore, their dress and behavior had grown so informal and diverse, as in the restaurant in Winnipeg where Mennonite matrons were once waitresses and now young women so "tarted up," as Sweeny put it, went around in sheer tops, with the buttons up the backs of their black skirts undone to reveal their legs, that it seemed they'd been hired at the university up the road. The men at the auction acted as acculturated; they asked the auctioneer for a break at fifty thousand and huddled, and Kiner, who needed air, walked out and heard one say, "But we need to get our equipment fixed when we want!," and then another: "But he's not here!"

"Why do you want to know who it was?" Kiner asked.

"Go offer it to him for his bid. If he's still a taker, you're only out the difference. Otherwise, you're out five-two. And there'll be another auction."

Kiner didn't think he could endure the loss or the shame of that, and then the person at the next table, a young man with side whiskers, turned and said, "I'll buy it. Sorry, I'm Ralph Kohl. I'll buy the shop and whole setup for what you paid, Mr. Kiner, and I'll pay back your five thousand two hundred, if you'll manage it for me—but *half* time. Just for a while, till we see how it's going. Six months, say, then we'll see. Your grand-dad used to shoe horses for my uncle and my dad, Mr. Kiner.''

The shop, of shining blue steel, was on a hilltop at the outskirts of town, and its crushed-rock drive gave out sounds like crack-ing ice as Kiner drove up it, and then Sweeny sat and exclaimed, ''What the—'' And at the sight of the building added, ''Oh, this crapulated mess!''

The only suggestion of a mess was the streak of black above the broad, electrically raised overhead door and a rough-edged hole in one of its fiberglass panels that had been repaired from the inside with Styrofoam, now gray behind the fiberglass. Sweeny got out and trotted to the entry door, to the right of the overhead, got it open with his keys, and stepped inside, leaving it ajar. It was Kohl who had authorized the group to bid, as it turned out, on a day when he couldn't leave the metal-fabrication business he had started in Winnipeg; this shop was to be an adjunct to that, besides handling the needs of local members of their sect. ''They should have bid on up,'' Kohl said. ''But you'll attract a different kind of customer. You'll be good, if you can work it out that this business, like all mine, is run on my religion.''

It was then that Kiner delivered his homily on business and religion, although exactly what Kohl's religion was, he couldn't say; he had taught and worked in a realm so refined beyond explicit religion that its presence in an actual person intimidated him.

The wind was worse on the hilltop, Kiner noticed, and there was less snow, but inside it was so cold that frost had formed around the door, and he was careful not to touch it with his coat as he pulled it to. The entire interior of the building, once with walls of shining steel, was so black it was like walking into a coal mine. The racks of steel ahead were furry with soot from burned rubber, and every surface was coated with blackened ash.

"The lousy coal furnace is out again!" Sweeny called from the far end of the building, where the bulk of the furnace showed faintly green through all the black.

"Get it going," Kiner ordered. A reserve gas-fired heater that hung overhead was going full blast, driving delicate black soot through the air. Kiner could already feel it on his face, like the settling of a grief he couldn't shake. Two weeks ago somebody had phoned him at home and said, "Your shop's on fire," and hung up. He thought it was a prank, but once he'd got to the car and gone past the elderly couple's corner, he could see black smoke rolling above the edge of town. He was convinced it was the fuel he had ordered for the furnace, trying to save on coal and be ecologically sound—a new product made of crushed waste formed into pellets ("Dog shit," Sweeny called it) that had never fed into the stoker right. Kohl had chided him for buying it—"Don't be penny wise and dollar foolish"— and now it looked as if it had cost them the whole place. But when Kiner pulled up the drive, trembling at the sight of firemen scrambling all over and breaking out windows, while yellow-black smoke billowed from the shattered and raised overhead door where a fireman's pike hung from the hole he had punched to raise the door after the electrical wires had burned through, Sweeny came hobbling up, one side of his hair scorched, his eyes red in his blackened face, and yelled, "I did it! Fire me!"

Had Kiner really taken Sweeny in his arms? It seemed so; the clothes Kiner had been wearing that day were ruined. "I tried to start the frigging forklift!" Sweeny said. "So I could move them bundles of steel that was delivered, and ran out of gas over at the side of the building." He pointed toward the welding tables, and Kiner saw that a swag of draped ceiling insulation had dropped onto the hydraulic press and melted, the heat twisting a huge girder above. "I siphoned some out of the mobile unit, since we had it in to sandblast them boxes, and filled up the forklift, and then Kohl called for you, and I know I should have put the gas can back in the cage where we keep them combustibles, I know it! But I figured I'd finish the weld on our truck boxes before I sandblasted 'em today—you said I should do that—but I left the gas can by the forklift, open, I guess, and with the first contact on that weld, a sheet of fire went across the floor to that forklift, *whoosh*, like a blowtorch up a nightie, and I think the tank on the lift went up, too. Shit!" He was sobbing and ran a curled burned hand over his black face. "I got the closest fire extinguisher, but just a squirt of baking soda came out of it like snail doodle, and the heat was getting so bad"—he held up his burned hand—"I couldn't take it, so I run out and tried to scoop up some dirt, but the ground was too frozen, and when I come back in with about a cupful, something exploded!"

Kiner sighed now, realizing he'd given the poor man too much to do, in trying to meet Kohl's deadlines. Sweeny had somehow made it to this end of the building, to the counter Kiner stood beside, now smeared black, and tried to call the fire department; the phone lines were burned out. So Sweeny got in his truck and raced to town and pulled into the closest place, a feed store, and the manager there called in the fire; later he said to Kiner, "Oh, was he scared, but if he hadn't left the door open when he ran, it might not have— But that's easy for us to say afterward, ey? It was those tires on your forklift that burned so fierce. Them and the oil from your hydraulic press when it blew."

Kiner went into his office, a cubicle built into the front

corner of the building—a tool cage attached to its back and a second story above, with enough room under the roof to store parts—and the phone on his desk, as if alerted by his presence, jingled. He checked his hand for soot and picked up the receiver. "Kohl's."

"Where were you?" It was Kohl, as breathless as if there'd been a further disaster. "I called at eight-ten."

"I left late. I had to give Sweeny a ride in, be—"

"What if a customer'd come to the place or called?"

"I think most everybody in the area knows—"

"You said you'd be in early after that fire!"

Kiner leaned his rump on the desktop, weak in his legs. The door to his office had been shut to the conflagration and spared the worst of the smoke and soot, but a fireman had broken its window and soaked the inside, dislodging and exploding the tiles of the suspended ceiling, and an inch of water was standing on the floor when Kiner had arrived. Kohl viewed his lateness that day as a lack of oversight that permitted Sweeny, whom Kohl did not admire, to ignite the place, since Kohl was already irritated at the fussy way the two were preparing the building for a grand opening; and Kiner was never sure how to sort all this or the tack he should take with Kohl, who had in one sense rescued him and now was smarting from his own loss.

"The agreement was I'd work half time. I've been in from eight to twelve hours a day since the fire. And till we learn the rate to feed those pellets into the stoker"—he pulled on the long cord of the phone so he could see out the door to where Sweeny was lighting the furnace, as usual, with an acetylene torch—"I've been coming in at midnight to check on it." Though he hadn't last night. "Sweeny and I have agreed that he'll open in the morning, but he had trouble with his truck. There's a storm—"

"I said I wanted you to run that business the way you thought it should be run, and I still say that. Not the way Sweeny does. I guess you missed the insurance adjuster."

"No," Kiner said, although he couldn't say for sure, of course. "Our appointment is for ten."

"Don't let him squeeze out of a dollar of it!"

"I won't. I have the estimates at hand." Kiner went to the desk and didn't see the file, a red one, that he had prepared. Was that what he'd forgotten this morning? He pulled open the top drawer, a side drawer, another, as Kohl went over details he expected Kiner to mention, and then Kiner stepped over and eased open the drawer of a steel filing cabinet that had kept their records mostly dry. "Is he there?" Kohl asked. "I hear doors opening and closing."

"No, but I better get ready." When Kiner hung up, he was out of breath and shaking. He found the file in the toilet off his room, where he sometimes hid. Then he heard Sweeny yell from the shop, "Hey, Mr. Manager, he's here!"

The adjuster, a young Toronto native with the look of a gambler alert to any scam, stomped his feet inside the door, sending slivers of snow scattering over the sooty black floor, where they smoked like dry ice. "Cold!" he cried. "It seemed a ground blizzard on the drive down, but it's climbing!" He turned to look out the reinforced glass of the entry door, and past his profile Kiner saw swirling snow. "Well," the fellow said, brushing at the dull light shimmering over his black-satin warm-up jacket. "Let's get to this, ey?"

Kiner wouldn't let him into his office; he saw this as his edge: have him sit where the damage was. Past the tool cage, in a corner where paint-spray equipment was stored, was a long hardwood table where Trotmeyer and Sweeny used to sit and eat from their lunch buckets. A dozen sheets of paneling were stacked on it. The day before the fire, Kiner had had the paneling delivered, intending to refurbish his office, and had had it laid on this table, sturdy enough to accommodate it, and had since covered it with plastic. He asked Sweeny to come over and help him flip the paneling, so that a clean surface was up, and to illustrate how many sheets had suffered soot and water damage, and sat the adjuster down at it.

The young man was surprisingly agreeable (when Kiner had reported early estimates, he'd cried, "But I told the office this was only going to cost them twelve thousand!"), and he accepted without comment a long series of estimates from Kiner, entering them on a balance sheet: cleaning the interior, rewiring the building, repairing the hydraulic press and forklift, replacing the ceiling and the overhead door, redoing Kiner's office and both toilets, painting the beams supporting the building, renting equipment to move everything out and renting space to store it, so the work could begin in earnest— Kiner came to painting the interior. "Seven thousand is the lowest bid," he said. "The others are for nine-one and eighty-seven hundred."

The adjuster tossed down his pen. "No way!" he said. "That's impossible."

Kiner shoved the papers over. "It's the industrial paint, which has to be put on in two to three coats."

"These walls weren't painted to begin with!"

"Everybody agrees that even a power washer isn't going to remove the smoke stains—smoke oxidation, they call it." Kiner looked up and saw Sweeny hurrying past the man's back, grinning and pounding a fist into his palm. "Imagine the gloominess of working in this atmosphere," Kiner said.

The adjuster glanced around, his canny eyes on Sweeny heading toward a welding table piled with tools, then turned back to Kiner. "Think existentialism," he said, and smiled. "You're the guy who writes about philosophy, no?"

Was this a new tactic? Kiner drew back in his chair, then said, "A book or two might still be in print."

"My wife's taking a night course on existentialism, and she said this Kiner I was going to see had something in a book her professor wants her to read, no?"

"It's the old guy!" Sweeny cried, and Trotmeyer came in the door, closing it softly behind him, and dipped his head in a birdlike way to peer past the gloom, the white hair under his engineer's cap sticking out in shocks and tufts against the winter light. "The same crapulated mess," he muttered. "Sweeny!" he yelled, and Sweeny came scuttling over as he never did for Kiner. "What have you been up to? Doesn't doing nothing get tiresome when you can't stop to rest from it? Are you going to clean this place up and get this business going or shut it down!" He went around Sweeny in catlike strides, pausing at the junk on the welding table, then headed toward the racks where bars and flats and shafts of steel were stored. "You'll lose the trust and faith of your public—a businessman with sand in his pants knows that—if you can't clean up your own mess!"

"We been working every day," Sweeny said, glancing at Kiner and trying to get a hand on Trotmeyer, to let him know others were there. "But you know every inch of every tool and everything in here is covered with this shit, sir."

"See that steel?" Trotmeyer said. "All new steel, ten thousand dollars' worth, starting to oxidize. It's Christ's ruin on it!"

Kiner wondered whether they were staging this for the adjuster—Trotmeyer hadn't glanced their way—and then remembered that on the day of the fire, as he worked with a squeegee to shove the worst of the water out, he had seen Trotmeyer appear like a prophet against the sky, coming through the open overhead door. Then Trotmeyer cringed, turning on his heels as if he would fall, and raised both arms and threw back his head and bellowed, "They've ruined my beautiful building!"

"What's this?" the adjuster whispered, studying Kiner.

"He retains a kind of proprietary interest."

Trotmeyer strode over to them, his eyes magnified to the flatness of fish eyes behind his glasses, nibbling on the stub of a smoking cigarette in a habit that had stained the stubble around his mouth yellow, and shouted at Kiner, "You haven't moved an inch on this mothering mess!"

"Oh, yes. First, we wipe everything with WD-40—"

"As every piece of that steel, by God, better be!"

"Yes, that will be done, and take days—a week. We're working right now on the insurance for the rest of it."

"Excuse me," Trotmeyer said. "I mean that. If I've become the kind of helpless old dip that starts interfering with real business, may my ass suck blue clay balls!" He went for the door, which Sweeny was hurrying to open, and then swung and shook a long finger at the adjuster, and said, "You cough up every cent! I've paid in fifty thousand in premiums these last ten years and got not one bean!" He grabbed a fire extinguisher and sent it skidding along the floor, sparking. "Check the tag on that! The son of a bitch who inspected it declared it perfect six months ago, and if it is, I'm an angel! Sue the bastard and pay these fellows double!" He went out and Sweeny shut the door, then reopened it and scrambled after him, closing it with a clong.

"The windbag," the adjuster said. "He's had this policy with us eight years, and this is the first year it went over twenty-two hundred."

"The interior," Kiner said. This was his lever, as he saw it; Kohl had said paint didn't matter that much, and a person Kiner trusted, an elderly painter who had worked with every sort of surface and building, told him no paint made would stick to galvanized steel. "Some company concocted a warnish once we thought would, but come ten years, all it's on the floor fallen." So Kiner pretended to sadly give up the painting, if two thousand was added, he said, to the cost of cleaning and moving everything out—one of Kohl's demands. The adjuster sighed. The total he arrived at on his calculator was twenty-seven thousand seven hundred dollars.

Kiner and Sweeny spent the day cleaning. They had been at this two weeks, and some days it seemed to Kiner, as to Trot-meyer, that they hadn't moved an inch. Everything in the place, though, from templates to bearings and sprocket gears and wrenches and welders and clamps and drills to machinery and chairs had to be cleaned of the clinging soot—particularly galling to Kiner, because over the weeks when they were preparing to open, he would come to the shop at night and sit and survey the beauty of the place, imagining his grandfather here, and walk around and wipe away even stray handprints from the walls. For this worse task, he wore the coveralls he had on. After the first day, they were too filthy to wash; he'd tried. And though he always wore gloves, his hands were gray and the lines in them like lignite seams.

"I'm sick!" Sweeny said. "It's past noon and my lunch bucket's in that damn truck! I'll have to unthaw it!"

Sweeny's alimentary system was as accurate as a clock, and now Kiner realized he'd been on his feet so long, on cold concrete, that he was chilled past his knees. He drew a twenty from his wallet. "Go get us something. Use my car," he said, and went into the office. He had put off calling Kohl, and now he got him on the phone and reported the settlement figure, without mentioning the amount he'd given up on the painting.

"Good going," Kohl said, but when Kiner hung up he sensed that the five thousand forgone—worse, not even mentioned—would, in the tangential effect of the two on each other, end their relationship.

Sweeny returned with a sack in one arm and said, "I saved you some bunch!" and handed Kiner ten dollars and a loonie, plus small change. They sat at the paneling and Sweeny flattened the bag and laid its contents on it—a loaf of bread, a bag of doughnuts, a chunk of liver sausage, a jar of mustard, two coffees each—and then slapped things together with a plastic knife. Kiner picked up a sandwich, trembling, and remembered his grandfather bowing over his food in silent prayer, then saw streaks of black from his fingers across the white slab of bread. *Good*, he thought, and was startled, expecting his mind to form "God." He felt cornered, in a worse retreat than any philosophy had caused.

Toward evening, when the windows of the building turned dark blue, Sweeny went over and switched on a partly melted portable radio suspended from a beam. Then, using his grimy industrial wipe, which was what they had to use to stay ahead of the soot (in spite of the cost and poor ecology), Sweeny cleaned his prints from the radio's surface as he stood listening. He turned to Kiner, his face smudged and streaked, and grinned. "It's on," he said.

Kiner rested his hands on a pile of shims he had wearied of cleaning, his legs numb. "I hear that."

"I mean action in the Gulf! President George B. of the U.S. just said, 'Go get 'em!' " Sweeny made wings of his arms and swooped toward Kiner: "Boomely, boom-boom, *boom!*"

"I'm appalled," Kiner said, and sat on the overturned bucket he'd used for soaking the shims in gasoline, and saw the faces of the students at the last seminar he'd taught, as if they were sitting around him now, waiting for his response. That year he'd grown so vague and fumble-tongued he had said, *Essence precedes existence*, and not one of them blinked. American youth! The big-nosed fellow so ambitious he seized on every question before it was fully out; the curly-haired one who seemed sullen and blank but turned in a paper so sensitively phrased that Kiner wept; the fresh-faced brunette with the stare that seemed to offer him, even at his age, free access, if he'd been fool enough to jump. And it wasn't just American youth, but Canadians and Brits and Arabs and others, too, who were lining up for what Kiner could only imagine as slaughter— voiceless under imperialism's advance.

"I thought 'God-dumb Sodom' would crack," Sweeny said, one of his names for Saddam Hussein. He found a station in the States that was reporting on the war full-time and sat on a welded tractor seat next to Kiner. In the growing dark they stared into the distance and listened, and at one point Kiner said, "Did he say hundreds of sorties?"

"He did."

"That means thousands."

"We don't have that many planes!"

"Lives." Kiner turned to the hydraulic press, like a black-ened gallows in the dimness, and heard *baldachin*. He was in London for the year and had walked down Whitehall to the Banqueting House, into its long, barren main room, with a wooden throne on a dais at one end, and tried to imagine a pageant by Inigo Jones, or Shakespeare's troupe enacting *Twelfth Night* for spidery James I, and was about to lie on his back in order to appreciate the Rubens mural on the ceiling, of *The Apotheosis of King James*, when a gaggle of Americans walked in with a guide who said, "The throne, with its canopy, or baldachin, embroidered at the center with James's crest . . ."

And Kiner had gone over to one of the west windows and stared across Whitehall toward the Horse Guards; two were standing at attention in scarlet tunics and black shakos in their stone niches, impressive at this distance—but nearly teenagers, Kiner had seen, when he had walked past. A draft seeped through the window that held his reflection, and the durability of the duty of those young men, and others like them, standing guard for centuries over the fortunes of kings, sent his philosophy—which had been not only his ruler and king, like the late James, but his god—into apotheosis, through the ceiling.

Kiner went to the office and turned on his fluorescent desk lamp. He had brought it and a padded swivel chair, once in his university office, to the shop before the fire, and the woolen fabric of the chair was now blackened beyond cleaning. He hadn't included it in the insurance claim. He sat in it and treadled himself backward and turned to the window. Rows of yellow lights outlined the town's streets below, and Kiner imagined the eruption of flame that had sent Sweeny fleeing there, then the explosions occurring at this moment across a desert country, as if ignited by this fire, and covered his face. He would stay with Kohl until the place was cleaned, period. He rolled himself forward and placed the agreement, signed by him and the adjuster, into the file of estimates, shoved it all in a drawer, and stood at the window. The ground everywhere was white, the wind down, and he thought, At least we're alive.

On the drive home, Sweeny fiddled with the radio until he had the American station and sat back, frowning in the dash light, as pilots reported on the effects of their raids. "Them electronics can get a duck up his gizmo," he said, but was subdued. By the time they got to his turnoff, the wind had picked up, sending sudden snow spouts springing up as if jerked by wires. Sweeny's stalled truck, centered in Kiner's lights, looked like a sinking hulk in its snowbank. "What's the problem, do you think?"

"Alternator," Sweeny said.

"Shall I call somebody?"

"The auto club'll get it. I pay them buggers more'n I do on repairs but always get it back. Let them unthaw it!"

Sweeny's house trailer, on open ground with shrubbery at one end, appeared to float and rock with the wind as they sat in the heated car and listened to a report of the first missing plane. "I don't like this," Sweeny finally said.

"I know." Kiner tried to form a comment of the kind he might deliver to a seminar, and then thought, It's the fire at the center of this winter that has brought us all down.

"Somebody's dying," he said.

"*Pfft!*" Sweeny went, and hopped out his side. He leaned into the interior light and gave the smile that set his eyes askew, and Kiner saw that even his teeth were dotted with soot. "Partner," Sweeny said, "I love ya!"

In his entry, Kiner pulled off his coat and boots and stepped into a side porch, where he'd set up his desk, and then back out, as if stung, to the wood stove in the hall, and held his hands over it. It was cold, of course, and the forced-air furnace didn't deliver the kind of heat he needed. He stepped outside and without a coat or cap felt the force of the wind. There had been a woodpile behind the house when he'd arrived, and after burning wood all last winter, he'd been too busy to replenish it, or to ask anybody to, and now he saw only a dozen scattered chunks, split logs, frozen down and mounded over by the granular snow.

He bent to dislodge one, and a gust of wind peppered his face with icy bits, forcing his breath down his throat, just as the wood came free. He stumbled backwards, trying to get his balance, and hit on the seat of his pants. And felt, in a backwash of age, that he would as soon not move. Which got him to his feet. *I love ya!* he heard Sweeny say. He loaded his arms with the wood, dazed, and carried it in, and stood stomping his feet inside the entry to restore feeling to them. He'd worn only his slippers. He ran a hand over his beard to remove the snow, melted to droplets. Local farmers used to build wood burners by fastening one thirty-gallon oil drum above another, to reburn the gases formed in the lower drum, the fire chamber, and Kiner's grandfather had gone the design one better by using eighteen-inch cylinders of steel, welding the setup together with a flat cooking surface on top. Kiner stuffed wads of newspaper into the firebox, got a blaze going to draw a draft, and then tossed in kindling he kept handy, then three pieces of the split wood.

He sat on the floor and stared into the flames, partly mesmerized, until his eyes dried out, and then shut the stove door. He worked around to the side of the stove, turned and lay back, resting his feet on the cylindrical firebox, his shoulders through the door to the porch, his head resting on its floor. In the dim light, the wood ceiling of the porch seemed the dome of his mind. Lying here his first fall, he'd sensed a concurrence between the two and decided to work in the porch. His father had lain like this, a laborer—a lesser man than his grandfather, Kiner used to think, since his father and mother and Kiner had lived here until Kiner's mother had died, and then his father had stayed on. But the records that Kiner's father used to pore over at night, once unearthed by Kiner, revealed that it had been his father's prosaic skimping that had kept the farm from going under, not his grandfather's heroic stance at the smithy.

His father couldn't abide superfluous, theoretical talk. *Work* was his word.

A globular fixture Kiner had attached to the car-siding ceiling (revealed when he removed a layer of old perforated tiles) looked perfectly centered. Kiner sighed. His anguish at having a father who didn't care one whit what he did had subsided. During his student days, he felt the pain would do him in, and sometimes now, alone in this house where all of them had lived, the scrape of his pen brought back that time in a seepage that threatened to undo the present. Here where his mother taught him to read and his father sat silent and his grandparents encouraged his precociousness, the invasion of the past kept up until there were days when he couldn't remember his age. His mind was not inviolable, he'd learned long ago, but that wasn't his concern; here, he didn't know how to justify the workings of his mind.

He had found a poet, not a philosopher, who said, "The most authentic philosophy is not in the objects of reflection, so much as in the very act of thought and its manipulation," and for a while lived by that, until he recognized it as merely another form of *process*. If your thought stuck on BBs, that was your authentic philosophy. As justifiable as imperialism. He worked himself to his feet, the soles of his slippers like heating pads now, and switched on the light in the porch. His antiquated typewriter sat at the center of his desk, the windows above furred with hoarfrost. Wood letter trays on both sides were loaded with papers, and a pile of mail stood as high as his typewriter. He sat in a swivel chair on casters, his favorite chair, firmer than the one he'd taken to town, and decided to try to begin by answering the most important mail first.

There were letters from a dozen academics, querying him on points in essays that he'd all but forgotten. A French publisher reminded him of a preface he had agreed to do, for the reissue of the French edition of his first book. Kiner's editor in New York had a similar request, but worse; this normally sunny aristocrat wanted Kiner to consider doing prefaces to all his books, "so we can start thinking about a uniform edition." A German translator sent six pages of questions on a recent essay. Kiner paused at a letter typed on airmail paper, thin as tissue, from a librarian in China, a woman who wanted him to send her two of his books and to help with her translation of his essay on the philosophy of economics, now that her country was, as she wrote, "broken unto pieces."

Kiner dropped her letter onto the stack and rolled his chair backward, and the momentum seemed to carry him over the edge of the snowbound world, past the pale of existence. Faint light sparkled across a car-siding ceiling, and heat spread from the entry over his back. Then a presence as powerful as his father, though smaller, smaller than Sweeny, came from the direction of the stove to the porch and settled in Kiner's lap. And he understood that he had subverted the child he'd been when he grew up here—that dim boy looking out with awe at his elders arranging the new world—and he thought, *Oh, my God. Save me from death.*